# BJ:
# ABUSE THROUGH
## The Eyes Of A Dog

# BJ:
# ABUSE THROUGH
## The Eyes Of A Dog

## STEVEN H. WOODWARD

XULON PRESS

Xulon Press
2301 Lucien Way #415
Maitland, FL 32751
407.339.4217
www.xulonpress.com

**xulon**
PRESS

Printed in the United States of America.

ISBN-13: 9781545632864

# Table Of Contents

# Preface

This is a heart warming book for all ages. It is a book of fiction where I have endeavored to place myself in an animal's world, through my own experiences with animals. All the names and places are purely fictional, except for the main character BJ.

However, this book is based on some true events about a real dog named BJ that was sent to me by God. He had been abused and I took him in when no one else wanted him. The dog on the cover of my first book, "Biblical Proof Animals Do Go To Heaven" is a real picture of BJ. If you look at his picture you will see that there is a Heavenly glow around his eyes and face. He was a beautiful spirit and he took me to Heaven.

Some of the incidents in this book are based on some true facts that I knew happened to BJ on his perilous journey to arrive at my doorstep; including the awesome divine experience that I had with BJ that I relate in my first book.

The purpose of this novel is to educate all people, young and old, that all animals are precious gifts and should be treated as such. I believe this story will bless the young and the old. This book endeavors to show that animals have feelings, souls, and should be treated with compassion. This book also tries to demonstrate to all people, that they can learn the qualities of love, compassion, forgiveness, companionship, and loyalty from animals. This book seeks to convey the fact that animals deserve the same dignity and respect as humans do.

I have always wanted to write a fictional story that included the importance of caring for God's animals. In several of the books that I have written, I have proved to the world that animals have feelings, souls, and that they do go to Heaven. Each of my last two books contains at least forty scriptures in each volume; for a total of eighty scriptures proving that animals are created, loved, sanctified, and blessed by God; and that animals are as important to God, as people are.

I pray that this book blesses all people with more compassion for God's creatures. I hope that you enjoy this book and that it changes you forever.

All my books are concerned with the treatment of animals:

*"Biblical Proof Animals Do Go To Heaven" by Steven H. Woodward.*

*"God's Revelations Of Animals And People" by Steven H. Woodward*

I give all honor and praise to the Lord Jesus for all my books; for without God I am nothing.

# *Dedication*

*I* would like to dedicate this book to Jesus and all the blessings and revelations that I have received in order to write my books.

To my loving Wife, Children, and Grandchildren.

To Lauren, Nicky, Liam, Gracelyn and to little BJ, who's life has inspired me to write.

And to all my readers and supporters; thank you.

"You can judge a person's character
By the way they treat an animal.
...And so does God."
-Steven H. Woodward

*Introduction:*

# The Beginning

*I* hate humans, and I don't trust them at all. They are the worst creatures in the whole world. Well…maybe not all of them. There was one that I really loved, but I crossed Rainbow Bridge yesterday and now I'm just hanging out in Heaven, waiting for his arrival.

My brothers and sisters that disappeared a long time ago are here too, along with my mother and father. I have many animal friends here, and even the humans are nice. Heaven is a wonderful place, and I don't have to worry about getting sick, hungry, or thirsty and best of all, no one hurts me here.

I have lived in many homes, and I have had many names, but BJ is my real name. It has taken me a lot of pain and heartbreak to get here, but… Oh…I'm sorry, I'm probably confusing you and you're probably wondering what I'm talking about. Maybe I should start at the very beginning…

## Chapter One

# *Runt Leaves The Farm*

*M*y mom said I was a pure bred Shih–Tzu, whatever that meant. My fur is grey-black and white. I was born on a farm and I was the runt of the litter; at least that's what the farmer's wife said. Farmer Sam owned the farm and he was the one that named me Runt; and that was the first name I ever had and this would be one of many names that I would acquire over the next few years. I didn't like that name at all and all the animals on the farm teased me about it constantly. When we were weaning, I always got the last bit of milk, but when we got a little older there was always plenty to eat for all of us.

There was a small pond where we would all go wade in the water and drink our fill in the shallow end. Before long, we had all learned how to swim and sometimes we would swim with the ducks. We splashed and played in the pond and took a bath whenever we wanted to. Life was good and no humans bothered us.

I loved the early mornings when the dew was still on the grass and we would all go out and chase the chickens. This always made the rooster mad and he would chase after us. We would all run away, laughing and hiding from him. We only did it for fun; just to watch the chickens run around and squawk. We never meant any harm.

The horses and cows were too big to chase and besides, they would only stand there and stare at you. Now the pigs; that was another story. You didn't mess with the pigs. Those pigs were crazy. They would try to eat you if they could, so we always left the pigs alone.

We would all run through the fields in the bright warm sun, playing and nipping at each other and rolling in the tall grass. It was a great life living on the farm, but after a while, strange things began to happen. Humans would come to the farm and fuss over us and talk to Farmer Sam, and then they would take one of us away. We would look for our missing brothers and sisters every morning, but we could never find them. When we asked our Mom where they went, she would just become sad and bow her head, saying that they went to live somewhere else.

Eventually, all of my brothers and sisters had been taken away and I was the only one left. It was an awful lonesome time for me because I missed playing with them. I used to wish that they would come back; but they never did. All that was left was me, Mom, and Dad until one day, Dad's life left him and Farmer Sam buried him in the ground. I heard Farmer Sam say that my Dad was "dead". I guess that meant that the life had left my Dad and I wondered if my Mom's life was going to leave too. There wasn't much to do by myself, but I still had a good life...until *they* came.

## Chapter Two

# Runt's First Home

M elanie and Glen answered the ad in the newspaper which read: "FREE PUPPIES". Their only daughter Cindy wanted a puppy, so they all got into their car and drove to the farm in answer to the ad, so that Cindy could choose a puppy to take home and call her own. Cindy was seven years old and she wanted an animal; preferably a dog. She had other pets such as fish and turtles, but they didn't do much except just sit there, or swim around in a circle inside a glass tank. She wanted something that she could play with and would be her friend. She wanted something she could dress up and take care of just like a real baby. Cindy's father Glen didn't care much for animals because he thought they were nothing but a nuisance and they smelled too, but he was willing to get a dog for his daughter. When they arrived and inquired about the ad, Farmer Sam pointed at me and said, "You're just in time, that's the last of the litter."

Cindy ran over to Runt and dropped down to her knees and exclaimed, "Oh Mommy I want him. He's so cute."

I was watching the humans and the little one came running up to me and I just stared at her, wondering what she was going to do. I wasn't sure what to make of this little human and I knew that every time humans came around, someone ended up missing.

"Awww. What's his name?" Cindy asked.

"We just call him Runt," Sam answered.

"Can I have him Mommy? Please, please, please!" Cindy begged.

"Are you going to take care of him?"

"Oh, yes Mommy! I'll feed him and take care of him, and he can sleep with me."

Melanie loved her daughter and she could never refuse Cindy anything. Melanie was a little dubious that her daughter would take care of the dog. She knew that she might be the one who would end up taking care of the animal; once Cindy grew tired of it, but...

"Ok Cindy, we'll take him home and see how it goes. However, if it doesn't work out, then we'll have to get rid of him."

"Oh boy, I'm going to name him Wiggles!" Cindy exclaimed with excitement.

5

I thought, Wiggles? What kind of name is that? That's worse than Runt! My new name was Wiggles and I hated it and I didn't realize that I was about to leave my beloved farm; just as my brothers and sisters had.

"Come on Wiggles." Cindy picked up her new friend and got into the car holding him in her lap as they drove away. As they left, Wiggles was shaking and whimpering from fear and Cindy tried to calm him down by petting his back and talking to him.

Melanie looked over at Cindy and her new dog and said, "It will take a while for him to get used to us and his new surroundings Cindy, so be nice to him. Right now he's scared because we're strangers."

I was scared and unsure of my fate because I had never left the farm, and I didn't want to leave my mother. I didn't know where I was going and I began to cry.

I was scared at first, but after several weeks had passed I was beginning to become adjusted to my new home, but I didn't like the male human that lived there. His name was Glen and I knew that he didn't like me because I could sense it right away, due to the fact that he ignored me and he never said anything to me.

"Just keep that stupid animal out of my way Cindy," Glen said after they had arrived home with Wiggles. "And if he bites anyone he has to go."

"Be nice Glen," Melanie said. "We have to give the dog a chance."

"Yeah," Glen replied. "He gets one chance and if he bites my little girl, he'll be sorry. I think this is a bad idea. She's too young to have a dog."

One day Cindy decided to dress Wiggles in her clothes. She had attempted this on several other occasions, but Wiggles had growled and snapped at her. However, this time she was determined.

I didn't want to wear human clothes and I had warned Cindy to stop several times before when she had attempted to put her shirt on me. I had warned her with growls and had even snapped at her to tell her to stop. I thought we had settled that problem, but she was trying to dress me again and I'd had just about enough. She tried putting a shirt on me again and I fought her by stiffening my legs and giving her a warning growl. Apparently, she didn't get the hint that I was completely against wearing any clothes.

"Now Wiggles don't be a bad boy. You have to put on your shirt and pants."

I wish this little girl would leave me alone. I don't want those strange things on me and I don't like this one bit. Please stop or I'll have to bite you.

"Sit still Wiggles! You're being very bad and if you don't sit still, I'll have to punish you."

After several minutes, Cindy became exasperated and gave up saying, "You're being bad Wiggles. Now I'm going to have to punish you."

Then Cindy hit me on the nose and I yelped and I instinctively bit her finger.

Cindy began screaming and cried, "That mean doggie bit me Mommy."

Melanie ran into the room and knelt by Cindy to examine her finger. It was only a small bite and a small amount of blood had formed around the bite.

Glen came storming in the room yelling, "What happened?"

"The dog bit her, but it isn't bad," Melanie answered.

I wondered why everyone was yelling. Did I do something wrong? I don't want to wear clothes and besides, it was only a small warning bite. Why is everyone so upset?

"That's it! I told you one bite and he's gone," Glen said angrily.

"Come on Cindy, let's tend to this bite before it gets infected," Melanie said.

Cindy was still crying as Melanie led her out of the room. Glen turned to me and said, "You're a bad dog."

I just stood there looking at him and I wondered what he was saying. I knew what the word "bad" meant and knew it wasn't a good word. Glen took off his belt and hit me across the face. It was very painful and I yelped and then I ran out of the bedroom door towards the kitchen, with Glen in hot pursuit. Glen managed to hit me again; this time across the hind part of my back, causing me to let out another yelp. Glen kept coming after me and he was screaming, "I'll beat you within and inch of your life you bad dog."

Cindy yelled, "No Daddy! Don't hurt Wiggles."

Melanie screamed, "Stop Glen, you're hurting him."

I slid into the water bowl accidentally and water splashed onto the floor. I then made a quick turn and made a beeline back to the bedroom. Glen's foot came down in the puddle of water that had spilled out of the dish and his leg shot out from under him and the other leg followed just as fast. He hit the floor on his back and it knocked the air out of him. I went through the bedroom door and jumped in the air, landing on the wooden floor, performing a

9

beautiful slide that took me under the bed. I was safe for now, but my nose hurt. I'm glad that human fell; it served him right.

"I'll pull all the teeth out of that dog's mouth," Glen said trying to catch his breath.

I thought, I wouldn't try that if I were you Glen; if you like using your fingers.

"No Daddy, no," Cindy pleaded.

"That dog's outta here," Glen yelled. "I knew this was a bad idea."

I stayed under the bed until I thought everything had calmed down and then I peeked out from under the bed. I didn't see anyone and I could hear Cindy and Melanie in the bathroom, but there was no sign of the man called Glen. I ducked back under the bed until I could find out where he was.

Glen sat on the kitchen floor for several minutes catching his breath and he was mad as all get out. "Stupid dog," he muttered to himself. He got up and grabbed the leash and collar that Melanie had bought for the dog. "I'm taking the dog to the pound where he belongs. Maybe they'll kill him, or maybe they can give him to someone else and he can be their problem. He doesn't belong around Cindy."

Glen went into the bedroom and tried coaxing the dog out from under the bed. "Here boy, here boy. Come on out."

Melanie said, "The poor thing is hiding under the bed scared to death Glen. Just leave him alone and maybe he'll come out on his own."

"I'm getting rid of him as soon as he comes out from under the bed. We can't have a dog that bites our little girl. He could have hurt Cindy really bad."

"I suppose you're right." Melanie hesitantly agreed and whispered, "What about Cindy? She'll be heartbroken Glen."

"We'll think of something."

"Glen, please don't hurt the dog."

"Alright, I won't; even though he deserves it."

"You promise for Cindy's sake?" Melanie asked.

"I promise."

Glen squatted down on his haunches and looked under the bed calling, "Come on boy, I'm not going to hurt you."

I looked at him and I wasn't sure if I trusted him or not. I was hoping that his head hurt as bad as my nose.

Cindy came into the room and asked sniffling, "What are you going to do Daddy?"

"I'm going to take him to the doggie shelter honey because he's too dangerous to be here. We'll get you another pet."

"But I want Wiggles," Cindy pleaded with tears in her eyes.

11

"Honey, Wiggles will bite you again, he's too mean."

Mean? I wasn't the one trying to put clothes on somebody. I didn't do anything wrong. Then I thought, he's going to take me back to the farm! Well, if I'd have known that, I would have bit Cindy long ago.

"Can I have a little kitty cat instead. They don't bite do they Daddy?"

"Yes sweetie, we'll get you a kitty cat, I promise. They don't bite. Now go on into the other room with your mother."

"Glen, don't tell them at the shelter that he bit Cindy, they might kill him. Just tell them you found him wandering around in the neighborhood." Melanie said.

Cindy left the room and now she didn't care if her Daddy took Wiggles away or not. He was a bad doggie and besides, she had changed her mind; now she wanted a kitty cat, because Daddy said that kitty cats don't bite.

Glen said in a calmer voice, "Alright, come on out boy. I won't hurt you."

I thought he was sincere and he wasn't yelling, so I figured that it was safe to come out. If he hits me, I'll run back under the bed again. I slowly and cautiously crawled out on my belly and stuck my head out to test the room. The human was squatting down and he wasn't making any threatening moves, so I came out from under the bed. I thought that he was going to take me back to my mother and the farm, and I was happy! I came out believing I was going home.

"That's a good boy," Glen said. He put the collar and leash on Wiggles. "Come on boy, we're going for a nice little ride."

Glen put Wiggles in the back seat and got into the car. He drove to the local shelter and once there, he took the leash and collar off the dog. He then took the dog out of the back seat and took him into the shelter. He went up to the front desk and told the lady he had found the dog wandering around the neighborhood and then turned around and left, before anyone had a chance to say anything to him. He left the shelter thinking that he would look in the paper and find Cindy a kitten.

I was happy to see him go, but this wasn't my farm! He must have made a mistake. Now I was in a strange place and I wondered how I was ever going to get back to the farm. Now I was trapped in here. I was trapped in jail.

## Chapter Three

# Wiggles Goes To Jail

They put me in a cell by myself and closed the door. I looked around and I was in a small narrow room and the floor was made of cement and it was hard and cold. There was a small opening towards the back of the cage that led to a very small space where I could see an old worn out bed. I didn't like this place at all, and I thought of my beloved farm and my brothers and sisters, and I hung my head and began to cry.

A strange voice asked, "What's the matter kid?'

I looked over across the narrow hall in the cell opposite of mine and I saw an old hound dog looking at me. He had brown fur, with a splash of white on his chest. His ears were long, and his face was droopy.

"Did you say something?" I asked the hound dog.

"Yes, I asked you, what was the matter with you; I could see you were crying," the old hound replied.

"Who are you?" I asked.

"My name is Old Blue. What's yours?"

"I ain't saying." I didn't want to tell him my ridiculous name because he would just laugh at me. Now I had two names and they were both stupid.

"Suit yourself. What are you in here for?"

"I bit a little human because she was trying to put clothes on me and she was hurting me."

"You didn't know?"

"Know what?" I asked.

"Humans can defend themselves, but we animals can't. If we do, they kill us."

"What does 'kill' mean?"

"You got a lot to learn kid. When they kill you, you are dead."

I knew what dead meant.

"Are the humans going to kill me?"

"Not if another human comes and busts you outta here."

"Busts me outta here?"

"Yeah, sometimes humans come and take you home with them to live. They let you stay here for a certain amount of time and if

15

nobody comes to bail you out, then they kill you. They're going to kill me because nobody wants an old dog. I only got a few more weeks left."

"Really? No kidding, they're really going to kill you?" I said with fear in my voice.

"It's ok. I'm old and tired anyway."

"Why are you here? What happened to you? Did you have a human?"

"Yes I had a human family, but they brought me here to die."

"Why?"

"Because they said I had become too old for them to have around and they got a younger dog in my place. Now a younger dog is sleeping in my bed."

"Oh, I'm sorry. Were they mean humans?"

"Oh no, they treated me wonderful. I had one those fancy double bowls that held water and food and I had a nice big bed to sleep in. Behind the house there was a big field with plenty of trees to run in. Yeah, it was a good life."

"I don't think I like humans very much. The ones I had were mean to me and the male human hit me. Worst of all, they took me away from my Mom and the farm where I lived. I was happy there and now I'm lost, and I don't know where my farm is."

"Sorry to hear that kid. Maybe a nice human will come and take you home."

"I don't know. So far they haven't been very nice to me. I just want to go home and be with my mother. I miss her terribly."

"Maybe someone will take you home kid. I hate to tell you this, but I don't think you'll ever find your farm again."

"Why not?"

"Do you know where it is?"

"No." I realized that I didn't even know how to find my farm and it made me sad. But I was determined to find it anyway. "Are the humans here mean?"

"No, they're really nice and they love animals."

"Then why would they kill us."

"You got a lot to learn kid. I'll educate you all about humans as long as you're here. Humans are funny animals, but like I said, I only got a few more weeks unless I get a reprieve; which I doubt will happen at my age."

"What's a re…re…reprieve?"

Old Blue laughed and said, "Yeah kid, you got a lot to learn."

The days went by, and Old Blue taught me a lot. He taught me about humans and a lot of human words, and what they meant. The people here were nice, but they didn't spend much time with us animals, which didn't bother me at all. As a matter of fact; I was just fine with that.

One day the human that worked in the shelter named Dave led Spike the bulldog down the hall. Spike looked very sad and he told us all good-bye. When I asked Old Blue what was wrong with Spike and where were they were taking him, Blue whispered, "They're putting old Spike down today kid." Blue had told me what that meant and that made me sad because I liked Spike. And after I thought about it, I got mad because humans could do this and we couldn't do anything about it. It just wasn't fair!

Humans came and went, looking for a pet to take home. Scruffy the French poodle was taken by a human family, and Midnight the cat was taken too. Blue and I told them good-bye and we wished them well. And of course, there were new arrivals too.

I remember the day Killer the Doberman came. He was raising cane with the humans and they had him on a long pole with a collar. Killer was mad at the humans and I didn't blame him. I kinda wished he could have bit them and escaped from this jail. They finally got him corralled in the cell and slammed the door shut. He jumped up slamming his paws on the cell door barking and snarling for a few minutes, and then he finally gave up. He looked over at me and angrily said, "What are you looking at?" I just ignored him and shifted my gaze elsewhere, because I knew he was just mad and that he didn't really mean it.

The humans had put him in the cell next to Old Blue and later, after Killer had calmed down, we asked him why he was here. He told us that he had bitten his human because the human kept beating him and he had had just about enough of that. He turned out to be a pretty nice dog once he got over being mad and I have to admit, it made me happy knowing that Killer had gotten some justice biting his human. Killer hated humans too just like me. Killer said he was going to make a break for it when he had the chance, but Old Blue whispered to me and said, "Killer doesn't know it, but they are going to put him down tomorrow, because the humans considered him too dangerous."

I was sad for Killer, and my hatred for humans grew a little more that day.

Early the next morning, they escorted Killer down the hall and he had no idea that he was headed to his death. Blue and I solemnly watched him go. Killer put up a good fight, but it did him no good. I cried a little bit for Killer. I really liked him.

## Chapter Four
# Another Home Another Name

*T*he following day, four humans came to the shelter looking for a dog. There were two grown humans and two small humans. The little girl's name was Laura and her brother's name was Vincent. Vincent was nine years old and his sister Laura was seven. They had come to pick out a dog for Laura because it was her birthday and she had been begging her parents for a dog for over a year.

I didn't like the little boy as soon as I saw him. I knew he was mean just by the way he looked at me.

They looked at all the animals and Laura liked me the best. The lady named Carmen that worked at the shelter took me out of the cell and into the little room where the humans waited. It was called the introduction room.

"Are you sure Laura? This is the doggie you want?" her mother asked.

"Yes Mommy, I want this one," she replied excitedly.

Laura's mother told Carmen that they would take the little dog.

When the paperwork was done, they loaded me into the back seat of the car with the little humans. I was sitting on Laura's lap and the one called Vincent reached over and pinched me real hard and it hurt, but I didn't bite him.

"Mommy, Vincent is hurting my doggie," Laura cried.

"Vincent stop that, you're hurting the little doggie," his mother scolded.

"I don't like this dog," Vincent said.

"This dog is not for you, it's for Laura," his mother replied.

"Shut up Vincent and behave yourself, or you'll wish you had once we get home," his father said sternly.

"Don't hurt my dog Vincent," Laura said.

"What's wrong with him anyway, he just stares at you. Is he retarded or something?" Vincent said with a smirk. "Laura's getting a retarded dog, Laura's getting a retarded dog." Vincent sang in a sarcastic voice.

His father was driving and he looked over his shoulder towards the back seat and said, "I told you to be quiet boy."

21

Laura's mother asked her what she planned to name the dog.

Laura said, "Let's see...I think I'll name him... Fuzzy... no... Fluffy."

Vincent laughed and exclaimed, "Fluffy? What a sissy name. He looks more like a Spud with that flat face. How about calling him Retardo." He laughed and added, "I think he's retarded."

"I'm warning you Vincent!" his father said angrily.

These humans were dysfunctional. That was a word that Old Blue had taught me. It means, well...it's kind of like those crazy pigs back on the farm.

"His name is Fluffy," Laura said happily.

"Fluffy it is," Laura's mother said with a smile.

I had a bad feeling about this, because I didn't like the little boy at all, and he kept staring at me like he wanted to hurt me. I began to wish I could have stayed in jail, because I thought I would be safer, and I was missing Blue already. I knew I wasn't going to my farm and I was scared. I didn't like these humans.

As we drove, I watched the trees flashing by the car window thinking that perhaps I had passed by my farm without knowing it, and wondering what was going to happen to me now. When we arrived at the house, Laura put the new yellow collar on me and fastened the tan braided leash to it that her mother had bought. Then she took me to her bedroom and put me into a dog bed and I just stared at her wondering what she planned to do next.

"There!" she said. "Now you are home."

Vincent came in the room and looked at Fluffy. Vincent thought that animals were just something to amuse him because they had no feelings and were stupid. And he most certainly didn't like Fluffy. The fact that it was Laura's dog made him even madder, but he would fix that sooner or later; hopefully sooner. Laura wouldn't have *any* dog if he had anything to do with it.

"Get out of my room Vincent!" Laura said, and then she yelled, "Mom!"

"Vincent! Get out of Laura's room now," her mother said in a loud commanding tone from the kitchen.

"Aw mom, I ain't doing nothing." Vincent left the room, but turned to look at the stupid dog and grinned. "I'll take care of you later," he thought.

I didn't like the look that little boy gave me. He reminded me of that last human that hit me. He had the same look about him.

After several weeks had passed, I was starting to relax and enjoy my new home. Laura was nice to me, but I still missed my farm and I was scared of Vincent.

23

One day, while I was lying in my bed in Laura's room, Vincent came sneaking in the door. Laura was in the bathroom taking a bath and Vincent walked over to my bed while I was sleeping and picked me up by the neck and started to squeeze. I couldn't breathe and I couldn't yelp for Laura to come and help me.

Laura had just finished with her bath and had come out of the bathroom, when she saw what Vincent was doing and screamed, "Stop, you're hurting him! I'm telling Mom and Dad."

Vincent let go and said, "I was only playing with him."

When Vincent finally let go, I dropped to the floor with a thud and I fell on my side catching my breath, but I got up quickly and ran and hid under Laura's bed.

"Mom!" Laura yelled, "Vincent is hurting Fluffy."

"What did your father tell you Vincent?" his mother said from the kitchen.

"I was only playing," Vincent responded in a pathetic voice.

Vincent abused me every chance he got. One day he came into Laura's bedroom when she was gone and put the collar and leash on me and said, "Hello Retardo, I'm going to take you for a nice little walk."

He walked me down the block and we went over a hill where there was a small patch of woods. Two of his friends were there waiting for him and they greeted him as we approached. "I brought the stupid dog," he said.

One of the boys had a rope and they tied it around my neck, and then he threw the rope over a branch of a nearby tree. Then they all lit up cigarettes and began touching the lit ends to different places on my body. I yelped from the pain, but I couldn't run or bite them, because the rope held me in place. I smelled my fur burning, and after they had their fun, they pulled me upwards with the rope and I began to choke as the rope tightened around my neck. I kicked and kicked, but my air had been cut off by the tightening of the rope and I began to get dizzy. I could hear the humans laughing and yelling and then I heard someone yell, "Hey, what's going on down there? You kids let that dog alone!" All of a sudden, I fell to the ground choking as they let go of the rope and I saw them run away.

When I looked up, I saw an old man looking at me and he took the rope off from around my neck. He took something small and black out of his pocket and he began to poke at it with his finger and then he began to talk to it.

"Hello, police? Yes, I caught some boys down below my house hanging a dog. He looks like he's in bad shape. Ok, I'll wait here until you arrive. What? Oh, my name is Dennis... Dennis Sloan." He then put the small black thing back in his pocket. I was hurting real bad and it was hard to breathe, so I just lay there and hoped the old man wouldn't hurt me.

He knelt down and said, "You alright boy?" and he stayed there until some humans arrived. I heard the old man talking to the other humans and they were dressed in funny blue clothes. I could hear them talking and I was beginning to get my breath back, but my neck hurt, and the burns hurt even worse.

"Where do these boys live sir?" asked one of the men in the funny clothes.

A small van came and they put me into it. I don't know what else they did or what they said, because everything went black after that.

## Chapter Five
# Back In Jail

W hen I woke up I was on a steel table in a strange room and I was cold. My neck hurt something awful and the few spots where the boys had burned me still hurt. My side hurt too where I had fallen when the boys dropped me.

There was a man and a woman in white jackets hovering over me and I tried to bite them, but I couldn't because it hurt too much when I tried to move. I would have bitten both of them if I could have. Then they stuck a needle in me and I began to get sleepy.

I passed out again and when I woke up I was alone in a room lying in a soft bed. After a few minutes, a woman with a white jacket came in and I recognized her. All the people here called her Doctor Vickie, and I knew I was back in jail. The man called Doctor Toby came in and looked at me too. I was hoping that they would put me in the same cell I was in before, so I could talk to Old Blue again, but they left me in the room by myself and I was there for several days while I healed. Doctor Vickie kept sticking me with that needle and I slept most of the time.

On the third day, Doctor Vickie came in and said, "Hello little fellow how are you feeling today?"

I just stared at her. If she put her hand near me I was going to try and bite her if I could. She picked me up bed and all, and carried me down the hall. I tried to lift my head up to bite her, but I was too tired.

"Easy boy, I won't hurt you. That little boy won't bother you again, I can promise you that. He's in a lot of trouble."

They put me in the cell next door to my old cell and I could see Old Blue across the hall. He was still not dead.

Blue looked over at me and said, "Hey kid! How you doing? You weren't gone very long. What happened?"

It was hard to talk and I had to talk in a hoarse growl and whimper. "That little boy tried to make me dead Blue."

"I'm sorry to hear that."

"Maybe they'll put me down with you Blue."

"No kid, you don't want that. You're still young."

"I'm tired Blue. I miss my farm and my mother and I don't know if I'll ever see her again. I wish I knew where my farm was, so I

28

could go home. Humans are mean and I hate them. I don't want to be around them anymore."

Blue hung his head because he felt bad for the poor little dog. He'd had a good life and was ready to die, but this dog was young and deserved a good home with plenty of love. He knew there were good people out there, but this little dog was having some bad luck.

"You've just had some tuff luck kid, that's all. Maybe the next person you get will be nice and give you a good home."

"I don't believe any of them are nice. They're just like those crazy pigs on the farm."

"What pigs?" Blue asked perplexed.

"Never mind," I said, turning over and falling asleep.

When I woke up, I felt much better and I stood up and walked over to the cell door looking out through the steel bars. More people had come to look at us and I had made up my mind that I was going to run away, the next time I had the chance. I wasn't going to live with any more humans and the next one that took me out of here, I was going to escape and go look for the farm. I wanted to see if my family was there, but there was only one problem; I didn't know where it was.

A woman inquired about me and the man called Dave who worked as a shelter aide said that I wasn't ready for adoption yet.

Another man came by my cell and looked at me and said, "What's wrong with him? Why does he just sit there and stare like that?" Then he slowly walked away down the hall to look at the other animals. I wanted someone to get me out of here, so I could run off and try to find my farm.

I would miss Old Blue though, because I was learning a lot from him. Blue had taught me that female humans were called women and male humans were called men. Blue said the little humans were called kids. I learned much about humans from Old Blue while I was in jail.

Almost two weeks had passed and an old lady came in to look at the dogs and cats. She stopped at my cell and looked at me for a while, and then she went on down the line. She took Casper the Siamese cat, and left. I didn't know Casper very well because her cell was up at the other end of the hall in a wire cage. I could hear her meowing at night, but I had never talked with her. She sounded lonely and I hoped that the old lady would be nice to her.

Everyday, the shelter aides would take some of the animals outside so we could get some fresh air while they cleaned our cells, but they would only take a few of us at a time. Blue and I had devised a plan for my escape while waiting for a time when we would be taken out together. He was a good friend and I really hated to leave him, because he and I had become almost like family.

It was a simple plan; my collar was loose enough that I could wriggle out of it and take off running. Then once I got free from the collar, Blue would kick up a fuss and act like he was sick; drawing their attention away from me, and I would be free to escape. It was a great plan and I could almost taste freedom. Then I would be free to find my farm and my family.

## Chapter Six
# The Jail Break

*I* waited patiently, and finally the day came when Blue and I were taken outside together. They led us out behind the shelter where there was a small field, and it was only a short distance to the woods in order to make my escape. I waited until I got a little closer to the edge of the field, and then I looked over at Old Blue and he bowed his head to signal that he was ready. I backed up quickly and wriggled out of the collar so quick, that the shelter aide named Dave didn't realize I had gotten free, until after I had started to run.

Dave yelled, "Hey! Squirt is loose. Get him!"

"Hurry! He's going for the woods," another aide yelled.

The woman named Carmen that had Blue on a leash yelled, "Something's wrong with Blue, help me!" Blue was rolling around on the ground and howling like he was dying.

One man ran over to help Carmen and the man called Dave began to chase after me. It was total chaos! Blue had done a beautiful job and I could still hear him bellowing, as I ran laughing to myself; knowing that we had fooled those stupid humans. I looked behind me and Dave was still chasing me, but he was far behind me, yelling for me to come back. I could tell that he was getting tired already; humans are easy to outrun.

I ran faster than I had ever run in my life and I made it to the woods before they knew what happened. I laughed as I heard Old Blue howling and whining. Boy could that old dog act! Those humans didn't know which way to go.

When I entered the tree line, I didn't stop until I was well into the woods. I found a cut in a dirt bank where a huge old tree had fallen, and I hid behind it. I waited for a long time, until I felt it was safe to come out from my hiding place. I looked around and I didn't see any of the humans, so I came out from behind the tree.

I looked around wondering in which direction my farm could be. I had no idea in which direction to go, so I picked a direction and began walking. The leaves were falling from the trees and the air was crisp, and I felt good. Once I came upon a pile of dry, dead leaves that the wind had bunched up over in a cul-de-sac. I ran and jumped into the big pile and I rolled around in the leaves for a while laughing. I heard the leaves crunching as I wallowed around in the pile. It felt good to be free! After I had my fun, I stopped and looked around, and then I became sad because I remembered how I used to play with my brothers and sisters on the farm, and I started to cry. I missed them so much, and I wondered if they had returned to the farm by now, and if they were waiting for me to come home. I was determined to go back and see them, and I wondered if they would even remember me.

I got up and shook the small pieces of leaves off and began to walk. I walked in the woods most of the day and by evening I came to a highway. The sun was setting and the horizon was red, and gold. The few clouds that were in the sky were dark blue with a tinge of copper. There were some cars and a few big trucks on the road, and I knew that if one of those things hit me, it would make me dead. Old Blue had warned me about roads and cars, while planning my escape.

I spotted some human houses far across the road on the other side of a large field. I waited until there were no cars on the road and I headed towards the houses to look for something to eat. Some of the houses were lit up and I knew that I had to be careful and keep out of sight, but I had to chance it because I was hungry. I knew wherever humans were; so was food.

By the time I had crossed the field, night had fallen and the stars were starting to sprinkle themselves across the black sky. I saw some big black round things in front of the houses and I walked over and sniffed them. I could smell food, so I jumped up at one of the black cans and it tipped, and then it came back down. I kept jumping into it and I finally knocked it over. There was a bag in the container and it slid out onto the ground and I tore it open, eating what little I could find. When I had finished eating what was there, I knocked a couple more over, and ate what I could find that was edible. I heard a noise behind me and when I looked around, I saw two animals with black rings around their bushy tails and black circles around their eyes. I remembered that Dad had told me that they were called raccoons, and they used to come around on the farm looking for food. They were staring at me and I figured they were hungry too. I had gotten pretty good at knocking the black food containers down, so I knocked one more down for the raccoons before I left. I was tired and I crawled under a car behind a house and fell asleep.

The next morning I was awakened by a loud sound that scared me, and I ran out from under the car just before it started to move. I began walking and I tried to stay by the side of the road next to the open fields and woods, just in case I had to run. I was certain that the humans were out looking for me. As I walked, I saw several mud puddles and stopped to get a drink before moving on. The water was brown and bitter, but I was thirsty from walking, so I drank the water.

Once, a car pulled off the side of the road just behind me. A man got out and began walking towards me yelling, "Come here boy. Come on." I spotted a patch of woods and I ran towards them.

Once inside the woods I saw some animals, but they didn't bother me, and I didn't bother them. I surmised that they must live out here in the woods. I eventually came upon a bunch of trees that were in perfect lines and rows and there were round food balls everywhere that had dropped from the trees. My Dad told me these balls were called apples. I looked up at the trees and I could see several apples hanging on branches. All of a sudden, an apple dropped and almost hit me in the head and it rolled on the ground a little ways from me. I walked over and sniffed it. The apple smelled good, so I ate it. The apples were lying everywhere and I ate until I was full. The apples were very good and they had water in them that tasted sweet, and I remembered eating these on the farm.

I saw some big animals with what looked like tree branches on their heads. They weren't paying any attention to me because they were busy eating apples too. My Dad also told me that those animals were called deer.

Seeing the apples and the deer, reminded me of my beloved farm and everyone that lived there before I was taken away. I knew we had apples and deer on our farm, so I thought; I must be close to my home! I began to miss Farmer Sam, Mom, my brothers and sisters, and all the other animals that lived on the farm. Why believe it or not, I even missed those crazy pigs! I knew I would never see my Dad again because he was dead, but I still missed him terribly. I began to cry, and I lie down in some tall grass and curled up. It was cold but the sun was warm on my fur and I fell asleep.

When I awoke the sun was overhead. I was rested and feeling much better and I was even more determined to find my farm. I ate a couple more apples and then I began to walk, thinking that if I just kept going I would find the farm and then everything would be fine. As I walked, I envisioned my return to the farm and how everyone would be so happy to see me, and I picked up my steps.

Towards the afternoon, I came upon a small brook meandering its way through the bare woodland. I watched as two squirrels quickly scampered around in the dead leaves, digging for acorns. As they moved from place to place, they made quick, loud rustling sounds in the dry leaves. I figured they were too busy to worry about me. There was a woodpecker drumming on a tree off in the distance. He would stop, and then start again.

I went up to the stream to get a drink and there was a small dead tree branch lying across the trickling stream. I saw a cavalcade of red ants marching in single file across the grey weathered limb, heading to the other side of the rivulet. I bent down and lapped up some water. It was the best water I had ever tasted.

By the end of the day, I had come to the edge of the woods where it met a small field of brown, dead grass. The sun was setting and the horizon was colored red like fire. The sky just above the red horizon was an aqua green, with golden streaks here and there. The few clouds that were left in the sky were dark blue and colored with a tinge of pink around their edges. The mountains to the west had become a dark purple silhouette and it was beginning to turn colder, as the sun disappeared behind the far mountains.

I saw human houses on the other side of the field and by the time I had crossed the field, night had fallen. The moon was behind the clouds and the deep shadows gave me cover. As I approached the houses, I could see that some of the houses had their porch lights on. I was tired, and I was hungry. I slowly, and very carefully walked towards the houses, keeping in the dark shadows so that no humans would see me.

I didn't see any of the round food holders, but I could smell them. I sniffed the air and followed the scent up to a white fence that surrounded a house where the scent was the strongest. The porch light was off at this house, so I decided it was safe. I peered through the crack in the fence and I saw a food holder, but I couldn't get to it. I walked around the fence until I found a small gate. I pushed it with my paw and it opened slightly, and swung back shut. I then nudged the gate open with my nose and walked inside the fence. When I had walked a couple steps further, I heard the gate shut. I went back and tried to push it open, but it wouldn't budge. I was trapped with no way out!

## Chapter Seven
# Escaping The Fire

*I* realized I was trapped inside the fence and I stood still in the protection of the shadows to see if anyone was around. I couldn't get out of the fence and I was hungry, so I decided that I would worry about getting out after I ate. I didn't see any people around anywhere, so I went over to the food container and knocked it over on the first try. I was really getting good at this. I could smell food in the bag as it slid out of the container onto the ground. I tore the bag open and began sniffing for something to eat when all of a sudden, the porch light came on and it shone directly on me. I scurried over to the fence and leaned up next to it, hiding in the deep shadows that were cast by the house.

The door opened and an old woman in a housecoat stepped out onto the porch. She was holding a broom in one hand, and a flashlight in the other.

"Who's out there?" she asked. "You raccoons get away from that garbage can. I've got my broom and I'll swat you."

I was trapped inside the fence and the old woman was going to hit me with that stick she had in her hand. I didn't know what to do, except to get ready to run around the yard until she got tired. I knew I could outlast a human, especially an old one. I would bite her if I had to.

The old woman turned the flashlight on and directed the beam towards the garbage can. She saw that the can had been knocked over and the bag was torn open. Then she began to scan the area with the light, and as the beam lit up the area where the shadows had gathered, she saw a miserable looking dog standing up against the fence shaking uncontrollably.

"Well I declare! What have we got here? A little dog! Now how did you get in here? I've been meaning to get that gate fixed. Come here little fella. Come here boy, come on."

I just stared at her and hoped that she would go away. I heard her calling me again, and then she made some smacking noises with her lips.

"Come on boy, don't be scared of me. I'll bet you're hungry and cold. Come on inside sweetie and I'll give you something to eat, and you can get warm. You look as though you're starved to death, you poor thing."

I'm not here to socialize lady, I'm here to eat. Is she trying to lure me over there so she can hit me with that stick?

The woman realized she was still holding the broom and she set it down, leaning it against the porch railing, and then she held the door open saying, "Come on in the house and get warm boy. I'm not going to hurt you. You're scared aren't you? Now you wait right there and I'll get you something to eat, you poor little thing."

I watched the woman go back inside and I stayed where I was, not sure what she was up to, but I was ready to run. A few moments later, she returned with a bowl in her hand, and a bowl usually meant food. She placed the bowl on the porch and looked at me.

"C'mon boy. Here's some rice and hamburger for you. I know you're hungry."

I just stood there and stared at her.

"You're a scared little thing, aren't you? I'll go back inside and let you eat."

I watched as the woman went back inside and I could smell the food permeating the night air, and it was a far better smell than what was in the round container. I stood still for a minute or two, deciding whether to chance walking up onto the porch to see what was in the bowl. Finally, my hunger overpowered my caution and I walked up the steps and onto the porch. I sniffed the food and I began to hungrily eat the food in the bowl. I looked up, and I could see her looking at me through the glass door. I continued to eat, but I kept my eye on her.

After I had finished eating, I hastened back down the steps into the yard and melted back into the shadows. The woman came back out and picked up the bowl and asked, "Want more?" She looked at me for several seconds and then went back into the house. She returned in a couple of minutes with the two bowls and set them on the porch. "I brought some more food and some water too. I'll just set it here on the porch," she said.

She then went back inside, watching me through the glass door and I decided that she wasn't going to hurt me. I cautiously crossed the yard and went back up the steps onto the porch and began to eat the food that she had set on the porch; watching her closely as I ate.

After I had finished, I went back out in the yard and stood in the light, looking at her as she stood on the other side of the glass door. She opened the door and held it open saying, "Come on boy it's warm in here. You can't stand out in the cold all night."

I stared at her and I figured I had no choice, because the night air had turned very cold and I was trapped in the yard anyway. So

I slowly walked up the steps and went inside, watching her all the while. I looked around the living room and I saw there was a blanket on the floor by a heater. She brought the bowls inside and closed the door and set the bowls by the blanket. She then walked across the room and sat down on a couch. I watched her for several moments and decided that she wasn't going to hurt me. I licked my chops and went over to the blanket and sat down facing her without taking my eyes off her, to see what she would do. She said, "Lay down boy and get warm." I continued to stare at her. "Are you a stray? You don't have anybody do you? I don't have anybody either, so you can be my new friend. I think I'll call you...Buddy. Yes, that's a good name because you're my new buddy. I have a son, but he only comes around when he needs something. I guess we're both on our own. My name is Claire. Glad to meet you Buddy."

She continued talking for some minutes. Most of what she said I had no idea what she was saying, but I sat and listened anyway.

Clair was seventy-five years old and held her age well. Her hair was silver and she had an air of elegance about her. She still got around well and she was proud of her independence. She was a tough no-nonsense woman, especially since her husband had passed two years ago. She spent much of her time alone and the dog was a welcome relief. She decided to adopt the dog and take care of it until, and if someone came looking for him. The dog was a miserable sight and he had an odor from neglect, but she would take care of that.

I didn't think she would hurt me so I lay down and enjoyed the warmth. I rested my head on my paw and relaxed, but I kept my eyes on her. I was tired, and somewhere I fell asleep dreaming of the farm. In my dream, I was playing with my brothers and sisters; rolling in the tall grass, chasing chickens, and swimming in the pond.

When I woke up it was morning, and I looked around for Claire, but she was gone. I saw a bowl full of food, and another bowl filled with water. I went over and lapped up some water and then I walked from room to room sniffing, and checking things out. I went across the room to the bay window and jumped up with my front paws on the sill. I looked out the window and I wondered where the farm might be. I saw a black van drive by slowly, and the two men in it were staring at the house.

After some time went by, I saw Claire pull up in her car and get out carrying several bags. She headed for the front door and I went and hid behind the couch, slowly easing my head around the end of the couch where I could watch her.

She came in the door and looked around for the dog she had taken in. "Where are you Buddy? I have some toys and treats for you. Are you hiding from me Buddy? You don't have to hide from me sweetie." She dropped the toys on the floor and opened a bag of treats, spreading them out on the floor by the bowls. She set her pocketbook on the table and then she went across the room and sat down on the couch.

I saw the toys and treats on the floor and sensing no danger I came out from behind the couch and walked over to examine them. After sniffing them thoroughly, I ate all the treats and then I turned to one of the toys and sniffed it, but I wasn't interested in whatever they were, and I looked back up at the woman.

"You decided to come out from your hiding place did you?" she said laughing.

"You are a mess Buddy. Let's get you cleaned up, and you'll feel much better. You need a haircut and a bath."

Claire went to the bathroom closed the bathtub drain, and turned on the hot and cold water spigots, adjusting them until she was satisfied with the temperature. She laid a green and white striped towel down on the linoleum floor. Then she went back out to the kitchen and pulled out a bottle of dog shampoo from one of the bags she had brought home with the treats and toys.

"Ok Buddy, we're going to get you all cleaned up, and you'll feel like a new doggie."

As Claire reached down to pick me up, I snapped at her and she drew her hands back quickly.

"My goodness there's no need for that!"

I wasn't about to let her touch me and I only warned her, but if she tried to hurt me I was going to bite her.

"Ok, we'll give it some more time until we get used to each other."

After several weeks had passed, she made another attempt to give me a bath. I let her pick me up and put me in the tub of warm water and it felt good. She used a blue plastic cup to pour water over me. She then squirted shampoo on me and poured water over me with the cup, which allowed the shampoo to soak into my fur. She did the same thing with my head. She knew not to get her hands near my face. She took me out and dried my entire body, but left my head and face alone. I was satisfied with this and I didn't have to bite her.

In the weeks that followed I was beginning to feel comfortable with Claire and it was nice living in the warm little house. At night she would knit while watching television, and I would lay by the heater on the blanket. It was a peaceful time, but I still thought about my family and the farm.

Claire would let me out several times a day and I felt safe being inside the fence. Several times I saw those two men drive by slowly in the black van and they looked at me. I could sense they were bad men. We dogs can sense these things. They looked like a couple of nitwits to me and I had the feeling that they were up to no good.

The weather had turned very cold and I was glad that I had a warm house that I could retreat to. After some time had passed, I was starting to enjoy my new home. I had begun to trust Claire a little and I allowed her to pet my back; but only when I was in the mood. I was still determined to find my farm and when I went outside, I would always sniff around for a way to escape. Sometimes, I wondered if I should just stay here with Claire, where it was warm and safe. To tell the truth, I didn't know where my farm was.

One night I awoke to a smell that reminded me of the time when Farmer Sam had burned the brush pile at the farm. When the fire began to burn the brush, the mice would scurry out from under the brush pile and all the cats would go crazy chasing them.

I sniffed the air and the odor was very strong. I slowly walked, following the smell as it got stronger. When I entered the kitchen I saw flames and I could feel the heat, as smoke began to fill the room. I looked around wondering what to do and I knew there was no way to get out.

I ran into Claire's room where she lay sleeping on the bed and I began to bark loudly. I stood up and began to paw the side of the bed trying to wake her up. I barked and barked. I continued to paw the bed and finally, she woke up. "What...what is it Buddy? What's wrong?"

It was then that she smelled the smoke and she jumped up out of bed putting on her house coat saying, "Oh my Lord, the house is on fire! Let's get out of the house Buddy. Hurry!"

Claire and I quickly ran to the front door and out into the yard and through the gate. She stopped just outside the gate on the sidewalk, turning and staring at the house fire. I continued to run across the street and I stopped at the curb, just behind a black van that was parked in the street. I was free. I stood in the shadows watching all the people as they came out of their houses to see what was happening. They were staring at the burning house and after several minutes I heard a loud, high pitched wailing sound. I looked in the direction where the sound was coming from and I saw a truck coming down the street with flashing lights. I heard Claire calling for me, but she couldn't see me, because I was in the shadows.

"Buddy, where are you?"

I heard her tell someone, "I know he came out of the house because he came out with me, but I don't see him anywhere." I heard her call me again, "Buddy come here boy. Where are you? That little dog saved my life!"

I watched as the house became engulfed in flames. I felt sad, because living with Claire was not so bad and now I had no place to stay. I began to wonder what I was going to do now and I figured this was a chance for me to go look for my farm. I looked up at the night sky and it was full of stars, and I wondered how I was ever going to find my farm. Where would I start?

Suddenly, something jerked me up by the scruff of my neck and shoved me into a bag and I was in total darkness. Whatever was holding me let go of me, and as quick as I could, I bit into it with all my strength. It felt like a human finger, and then something hit me on the side of the head, and I lost consciousness...

## Chapter Eight

# Kidnapped!

*D*irty Bob and Willy had seen the dog in the old woman's yard several times while riding by in their black van. They had been casing her house for a few months now, thinking that an old woman like her probably didn't believe in banks, and was keeping a large sum of money somewhere hidden in the house. They knew she lived alone, but the problem was; the old woman hardly ever left the house, and now she had a dog.

Everyone called him Dirty Bob because he had no values or morals and he didn't care who he hurt, as long as he came out on top. He wore a black leather jacket and old worn out blue jeans. His black biker boots were shabby and his long black hair was tied back in a pony tail. There was an earring in each ear and one in his nose.

His sidekick Willy had the brain the size of a pea and he did whatever Bob told him to do. Willy was a skinny man with a hawkish face. He had a long nose and his brown eyes were big and round. He wore a blue faded ball cap to hide his balding head, and his Adam's apple protruded out so much, that it looked as though he'd swallowed a ball bearing.

Bob had decided to steal the dog, because in his mind it meant instant money, and he needed money right now. Dirty Bob told Willy that the dog in question was a pure bred Shih-Tzu and was probably worth some money. They had given up on the idea of breaking into the old woman's house for now. Instead, they had settled for stealing the dog and when Bob had seen the dog run behind the van, he decided the time was now. Bob needed money, and he was desperate. They had seen the house on fire and had pulled over to the curb to watch, thinking that maybe they would benefit from the house fire, once the people had left. They saw the old woman come out of the house followed by the dog. They watched as the old woman and the dog came out of the gate and onto the sidewalk. When Bob saw the little dog run behind the van, he told Willy to grab the canvas bag they used for transporting stolen items. He quickly told Willy his plan, which was to quietly sneak around the side of the van, grab the dog by the back of his neck, and shove the dog into the bag.

Willy was a little hesitant. "Does he bite?"

"How do I know moron," Bob replied. "I'll hold the bag open and you grab the dog and stuff him in the bag. Then I'll throw him into the van and we'll be outta here."

Willy looked down at the floorboard and said, "What if he's a biter? Why can't I be the one to hold the bag?"

"What's the matter Willy? Are you afraid of a tiny little doggie?" Bob said mimicking a little child's voice.

"No, I ain't afraid of a little dog. It's just that...what if someone sees us? There's a lot of people out there Bob."

"No one will see us because they are all watching the fire. That ain't her dog. She found it and it don't belong to anybody, so it ain't stealing."

"Ok...I guess so."

Bob said, "Now Willy you get out and be real quiet like. Don't shut the door or make any noise. I'll come around the front of the van and we'll sneak around to the back of the van and snatch the dog. I'll hold the bag open and you shove him down in the bag, then I'll throw him in the van, and we'll take off. Nobody's gonna notice us, because they're all too busy watching the fire."

They got out of the van and quietly tip-toed towards the back of the van where the dog was. Willy peered around the back of the van and saw the dog standing there looking at the fire. He heard the old woman calling for the dog and he waited for her to turn back and look at the house.

"I don't know where the poor thing ran off to. Buddy!" she said looking around. "Here boy. Oh my, he's gotten himself lost," she turned to look in the yard to see if Buddy was in the yard hiding somewhere. "Buddy where are you? Are you hiding in the yard?" she said, scanning the yard looking for Buddy.

When the old woman turned back to look in the yard, Willy made his move. He quickly grabbed the dog by the back of the neck and just as quickly, he shoved him into the open bag that Bob was holding. As Willy let go of the dog's neck and began to draw his hand out, the dog bit into his finger and he stifled a scream.

"He bit me Bob! That stupid mutt bit me!" he whispered loudly.

Willy punched the bag as hard as he could and the dog quit struggling.

"Be quiet and get in the van," Bob hissed angrily.

Bob opened the sliding door quietly, just enough to throw the dog into the back section of the van. Willy climbed into the passenger side holding his finger, muttering something under his breath about the dog. Bob shut the van door carefully, looking around to see if anyone had noticed them and seeing no one, he walked around to the driver's side of the van and climbed in. He started the engine and they roared off amidst all the confusion that had resulted from the burning house, just as the fire truck pulled up.

"That old woman will think the dog ran off," Bob said smugly.

"My finger's bleeding bad Bob."

"Oh shut up you little sissy."

"It hurts something awful Bob." Willy whined.

"Quit crying Willie, you sound like a sissy."

"I ain't no sissy Bob," Willy said in a hurt voice. "That fleabag bit me hard. He's got some awful sharp teeth on him. My finger feels like it's been cut with a chainsaw."

"Suck it up Willy. We'll take the dog to Ben's and you can take care of your finger there. Maybe Ben will buy it, or know somebody who will, and we'll get some money for the dog. That should cheer you up."

"It really hurts Bob. I should kill that dog for biting me," Willy pouted. "I think I need stitches."

"No, you ain't killing nothing until I get my money, and then you can go find the dog and kill him if you want; but for now, you treat that dog like he's your mama."

Ben's small, rundown house was located at the end of an old highway that was rarely used any longer. Ben was a big burly man, with a deep gruff voice. He had small eyes set in a big round bearded face, and he had little patience with most people; unless there was money involved.

Bob and Willy arrived at Ben's house and knocked on the door. Ben peered out the curtain to see who it was and after seeing it was Bob, he opened the door. Bob and Willy greeted Ben and then they all went into the living room, with Dirty Bob carrying the bag, holding it away from his body.

"What's in the bag Bob" Ben asked with suspicion. "I hope it's something worth my time, and why are you holding that bag out like it's gonna bite you?" Ben said laughing. He knew these two were idiots, but sometimes they stole some good stuff and Ben always paid them much less than what the items were worth; making a good profit.

"That's because it does bite," Willy said, showing Ben his bleeding finger.

Ben said in a gruff voice, "Go over to the sink with that finger Willy, you're bleeding all over my floor you idiot."

Bob said, "Ben, I got something worth a lot of money in this bag. It's a pure bred."

"Pure bred? Pure bred what? Talk English Bob."

"It's one of them Shih-Tzu dogs and it's probably worth a lot of money."

"Have you lost your mind?" Ben said incredulously.

"What do you mean?"

"I don't deal in live items."

"Just look at him Ben, he's probably worth a hundred dollars or more, and I only want fifty."

Ben looked at them both and said nothing, but he was curious and said, "Let me see it, maybe it is worth a little something." Ben couldn't believe how stupid these two were.

"Be careful Ben he bites like the devil." Willy warned as he stuck his finger under the faucet, trying to stop the blood flow. Willy had found an old rag in the van and had wrapped his finger with it, but it wasn't helping any.

Bob carefully opened the bag and Ben bent down towards the opening in the bag to peer inside. The dog tried to jump up and bite him and Ben jumped back. "Get that fleabag out of my house. Ain't nobody gonna buy that nasty looking thing and you better not have brought no fleas into my house Bob."

I was mad clear through and I wanted to bite all of them. I just wanted one chance and when I saw that human face looking at me, I jumped up and tried to bite it, but I missed.

Willy had stopped the bleeding and had wrapped his finger up with the rag again. He walked over to where Ben and Bob were standing.

"Mean little thing ain't he?" Ben said looking at Willy's finger smiling. Ben was glad the dog had bitten Willy and he hoped the dog had given Willy rabies.

"You don't wanna buy him Ben?" Bob asked.

"No, I don't want to buy him."

"Well, do you know anyone that would?"

"No! Now take that mutt and get outta my house!" Ben said in a loud angry voice. "You're wasting my time. Come back when you got something worth buying and make sure it ain't anything that's alive either!"

Bob and Willy took the bag and left. As they were getting into the van Willy said, "What are we going to do now Bob?"

"I don't know."

Bob put the van in gear and pressed down on the gas pedal as they turned out onto the lonely highway. As they drove down the road, Willy asked with excitement, "Can I kill the mutt now? How 'bout I just sling it out the door?"

"Well…we ain't gonna get nothing for it so it's useless to us, and we ain't taking it home with us. I don't care what you do with it Willy."

Willy jumped around in his seat excited at the idea of payback for getting bit. "I'm going to sling him out of the van while we're moving and we won't even have to stop. We'll just keep getting it on down the road. It'll be good-bye to bad rubbish as my momma used to say," Willy said laughing.

"Yeah, get rid of him, he's worthless to us," Bob said.

Willy climbed around the seat and went to the back section of the van where the dog was and grabbed the bag. He was laughing at the thought of tossing the bag and its contents out on the road and watching it bounce. The dog was kicking and snarling as he lifted the bag. "This dog's going for a ride he'll never forget." It was payback time he thought gleefully. Willy slid the van door open and with a big smile on his face, he slung the bag up and out into the cold evening twilight, as the van took the sharp curve.

"Not yet Willy, a car's coming!" Bob shouted as he wheeled into the bend of the road and saw a vehicle coming in the opposite direction headed towards him.

It was too late. The bag sailed high up into the air and when it came down, it landed onto the oncoming car's hood with a loud thump, bounced off, hit the pavement, and rolled over to the side of the road onto the graveled shoulder.

Buddy experienced pain like he had never experienced in his life and then everything went dark.

## Chapter Nine

# Buddy Dies

*R*onald and Beth were on their way home after having dinner with some friends. Ronald had taken a short cut on the old highway that was rarely used since the construction of the new highway. They had just entered the sharp curve in the road and were about to pass an oncoming black van, when they saw a man throw a bag out of the open door of the van.

"Look out!" Beth yelled.

Ronald swerved too late and the bag landed on the hood of their car with a loud thud and bounced off onto the other side of the road. He slammed on the brakes and the car came to a screeching halt. Ronald and Beth just sat there staring at each other with both their hearts beating hard, as the black van sped off down the road.

Finally Ronald asked, "Are you alright?"

She replied in a shaky voice, "Yes, I think so. Are you?"

"Yes, I'm just a little shaken up…what was that?"

"It looked like a bag of some kind. I think someone threw a bag of trash at us," she replied.

"No, I don't think so, because it was too heavy and solid for a bag of trash. Should we go see what it is?"

"I don't know Ronald, I'm scared. It could be anything."

"Maybe," he said thoughtfully. "Maybe I should go look."

"No Ronald let's just go home. It could be something dangerous."

"You think we should call the police?"

"Yes, but from the safety of our house."

Ronald thought about it for several seconds and put the car in drive. He started to press on the gas pedal, but then put the car in park. He opened the car door and got out.

"What are you doing Ronald?" Beth asked in a scared voice.

"What if we call the police and it turns out to be a bag of trash? We'll look foolish. Just let me go and check it out."

"No Ronald! Please come back," Beth pleaded.

"I'll be careful don't worry. I'll be back in a second, just wait here."

"No Ronald! Please come back," Beth pleaded.

"I'll be right back."

When he got out of the car he could see the bag lying on the side of the road in the gravel and he began to slowly walk towards it. He wondered what was in the bag and for some reason he just had to find out. As he approached the bag he thought he saw the bag move slightly. Was his imagination playing a trick on him? Then he saw the bag move slightly again. "Oh my God," he thought. "There's something alive in the bag!"

Ronald ran to the canvas bag and squatted down loosening the drawstring on the old sack pulling the opening apart, until he was able to look down inside the bag. What he saw broke his heart. He yelled to Beth, "Beth come quick."

"What is it Ronald?" she yelled, but he didn't hear her.

Beth had locked the doors and had turned around in the seat holding her cell phone watching Ronald, ready to call for help at any minute. She unlocked the door and opened it, stepping out onto the gravel she yelled again, "What is it Ronald?"

"You won't believe it! It's a dog, and I think it's still alive."

Beth ran to where Ronald was, her shoes crunching on the gravel as she ran to see what Ronald had discovered. "A dog?" she said with disbelief. When she looked into the bag she exclaimed, "Oh my God Ronald, the poor thing looks dead. What horrible person could do something like this? What should we do?" Beth began to cry and exclaimed, "What are we going to do?"

"I think there's an animal hospital just up the road. Let's take him there, maybe they're still open," Ronald said hopefully.

Beth cried, "Let's hurry, maybe he's still alive."

Ronald scooped the dog up and they ran back to the car. Beth opened the back door and Ronald placed Buddy gently on the back seat. They hopped into the car, made a quick U-turn, and sped off down the road as fast as they could go.

I regained consciousness for several seconds and everything was fuzzy and dark, and I was in horrible pain, and I could hear some humans talking. I figured they were here to make me dead and I was too tired, and in too much pain to do anything about it. And besides; I just didn't care anymore. Everything went dark again and I drifted into a strange dream.

Ronald and Beth headed down the road as fast as they could, hoping to reach the animal hospital as soon as possible before the little dog died.

There were only three houses that remained on the south end of the old road, and one of them was occupied by Doctor Toby Dixon and his wife Vickie. They were both veterinarians, and they ran the local county Veterinarian Shelter and Hospital that was next door to their house. It was the only animal hospital for thirty miles and it operated on county and state funds; and any and all donations were gladly accepted. Everyone at the shelter called Toby, "Dr. Toby" and everyone called Vickie, "Doctor Vickie". He and Vickie were both passionate about animals; however Dr. Toby was a realist. Doctor Vickie on the other hand, was more of a dreamer. She thought that she could save every animal that came to the shelter which Dr. Toby knew was not possible, due to limited funds.

They had kept Old Blue for as long as possible, but his time was just about up. Everyone at the shelter loved Old Blue because he was old, and he was no trouble at all. He had been at the shelter longer than any other animal. Toby, Vickie, and all the people that worked at the shelter had donated some of their own money to keep Old Blue alive a little longer, in hopes that he would find a home; but no one seemed to want him. It looked as though he would never find a home because of his age, and his time was getting short. They would eventually have to put him down due to lack of funds.

Dave was an assistant veterinarian and he only had a year to go in school and upon graduating, he would be a full fledged veterinarian. He loved working at the shelter and loved animals more than he cared for some people, and he had committed his life to helping animals. He was in charge of euthanizing the animals which was a job he hated, but he told everyone that if it had to be done, then he wanted to be the one to do it. That way he *knew* that it would be done in a humane and gentle way. He loved Old Blue with all his heart, and when it came time to put him down, Dave wasn't sure if he could do it.

Doctor Toby and Doctor Vickie were about to leave the shelter and go home, when a car came speeding up the road towards the shelter at an excessive speed.

"Who's that driving like a maniac? He could kill somebody," Dr. Toby said.

"I don't know." Vickie replied, watching the speeding vehicle as it headed towards the shelter.

The car slid into the shelter and up to the front door, and a young man and a young woman jumped out of the car.

"Hey, what do you kids think you're doing? You could hurt someone driving like that." Toby yelled.

"We have a hurt dog here that's been hit by a car. He needs help mister," Ronald yelled.

Vickie noticed that the young woman was crying and wringing her hands. She kept repeating, "It wasn't our fault. It was an accident."

"Get him inside." Dr. Toby told Ronald.

"Who are you?" Ronald asked.

"I'm one of the Doctors here at the shelter."

"Help this poor dog Doc," Ronald begged.

"What happened?" Vickie asked.

"We were driving down the old highway a few miles back, and a black van went past us and someone threw him out the door, and he landed on my car. I feel so bad, please save him Doctor," Ronald said almost crying.

They entered the building with Ronald carrying Buddy in his arms and Doctor Toby said, "Third door on the left, hurry!"

Ronald took the dog into the room and Vickie directed him to put the dog on the steel table in the middle of the room. Vickie and Toby began to work on Buddy while Dave took Ronald out of the room and shut the door.

"I don't think there's too much we can do for him," Doctor Toby said, "I think he's dead. There's no pulse, no heartbeat, and he isn't breathing."

"I'm going to start CPR," Vickie said with determination.

Toby watched as she blew air into the dog's nose, which she kept up for almost half a minute. Afterwards, she placed her hands on the dog's side and pumped up and down ten times. She checked to see if his heart was beating with no results, and then she pumped again, but the dog showed no reaction. Vickie yelled, "Come on boy! Toby, get the defibrillator and set it to ten joules," Vickie ordered.

"Vickie he's dead," Toby said with exasperation. "There's nothing you can do for him. You've tried CPR and that didn't work. Look at him, no dog can survive those wounds; especially that head wound. It would take a miracle."

"Toby don't argue with me and get the machine over here now!"

Doctor Toby breathed a loud sigh and pushed the machine over to where Vickie was. He switched it on and dialed it to ten joules. Vickie squirted gel on the paddles and pressed them together rubbing them in a circular motion, spreading the gel. The machine began to build a charge with a high pitched sound.

When the light came on, Toby said, "Ok, hit it!"

Vickie placed the paddles on the dog's side and hit the switch. Zap! Nothing.

Vickie tried three more times with no success.

"It's alright honey; he's gone to Rainbow Bridge."

Vickie had tears in her eyes and asked Toby, "Don't you recognize this dog?"

"No, he's such a mess I don't recognize him. Why?"

"This dog has been in and out of here several times in the past year or so. We called him Squirt, remember?"

"Oh yes, I recognize him now. He's quite a mess, and it looks like he's been through it a time or two."

"A time or two?" Vickie said, "I think he's been through hell and back. Poor thing," Vickie said through tears.

"Isn't he the one that escaped?" he asked.

"Yes, he's a smart little dog, and I think Old Blue helped him make his getaway with that phony sick act he pulled when this dog escaped."

"Oh, come on Vickie, do you really think this dog and Blue conspired together to plan this dog's escape?"

"Yes I do," Vickie said sniffling.

"What's wrong with you?"

"I don't know; there's just something about this animal that upsets me and I don't know why. It's as though...he's special or something," she said gazing at the dog. "I want to be alone with him for a few minutes if you don't mind Toby," she said.

"Why?"

"If I tell you, you'll just laugh at me."

"No I won't, tell me."

"Well...I feel like God wants me to pray for this dog."

"No, I am not going to laugh at you, I'm going to call a psychiatrist," Toby said.

"I'm serious Toby, I know you don't believe in God like I do, but please allow me my beliefs."

"Alright, I just hate to see you get disappointed, that's all. If you bring him back to life with prayers, then you'll make a believer out of me; that's for sure."

"Promise?" she said with a smile.

"Promise," he said returning the smile. "You're a strange woman Vickie," he said affectionately.

"Well, I guess that's one of the reasons you married me." Then she pointed at the door and said, "Go."

"I'll close the door and give you some privacy."

Toby left the room and closed the door. Vickie turned to the dog and put her hands on his side and began to pray. "Lord, let this dog live again. I know he's had a horrible life, so please just grant me this one request. Do it for me and this poor little dog, Lord. He's one of your creatures, please have mercy on him. I feel as though you want me to pray for this dog, and I am. I ask that you bring the life back into this dog once again. Give him a chance to be loved. Bring his spirit back Lord."

She waited, staring at the little dog for several seconds and then as she started to turn and leave, she heard the animal cough, then he choked, and then he began gagging. After a moment, he began to breath. "Praise God!" she said and ran to the door and threw it open yelling, "Toby, come quick; you got some patching up to do! The dog came back; he's alive!"

## Chapter Ten

# Buddy Has An NDE

W hen I opened my eyes I was in a strange place that I didn't recognize. I looked down and I realized that I was standing on a beautiful bridge. I looked in front of me and I saw a swirling mist that was a golden hue in color, and I realized that I was lost and I had no idea where to go, or what to do. I looked around and all I could see was the golden mist swirling around me like fog.

"Hey Runt!" a voice called out of the mist somewhere in front of me. That sounded like my oldest brother Charlie! Then another voice I recognized said, "C'mon and play with us Runt." That sounded like my sister Co-Co.

I thought I was losing my mind because I knew this wasn't the farm; but where was I?

"Who's there? Are you a human?" I asked, unsure of who it was.

"No Runt it's us, your brother and sister," Charlie answered. "Come and play with us."

"I'm here too Runt."

"Dad!?

"Where are you? I can't see you." I said.

"Walk off the bridge into the mist and you will see us." Dad said.

"Is this a human trick to hurt me?" I asked timidly.

"No Runt, it's us; Charlie and Co-Co, and Dad is here too. Come and play with us." Charlie answered.

"How can that be?" I asked in amazement.

I heard laughter and I figured that I had nothing to lose, and it did sound just like Dad, Charlie, and Co-Co. There was no where else to go, so I walked off the bridge towards the voices. I hated to leave the bridge because it was so beautiful, and I was a little frightened.

"Here I come," I shouted. "If you're humans trying to trick me I'll bite you," I warned.

Then I realized I wasn't in any pain and as a matter of fact; I felt great! I looked down at the pathway of the bridge and it was emerald green and it was as smooth as glass. There were tiny silver specks everywhere and they were scintillating like miniature stars. I turned and looked up behind me and there was a huge sign over the bridge that read, "Rainbow Bridge". Each letter was a different color and the letters shimmered and sparkled.

I walked off the bridge ready to fight any humans that I had to, as I headed towards the direction of the voices. I walked slowly forward expecting the worse. Suddenly, I came out of the strange golden mist and I found myself in a beautiful field, and there stood my Dad, my brother, and my sister. As I looked around I could see many other animals of all types. There were dogs, cats, gophers, squirrels, deer, and animals I had never seen before. I was shocked and happy at the same time. I thought maybe I was back at the farm, and I said, "Farmer Sam has really fixed the old farm up nicely."

They all started laughing and Charlie said, "Runt your not on the farm, you're in Heaven." Then they all laughed again and to my surprise, some of the other animals jumped up into the air and flew away.

Charlie's black and white fur was beautiful and glowing. Co-Co's tan and white fur was radiating with the same glow and I just stared in wonder. Dad had the same radiant glow and he looked so young! Finally I said, "You guys are so beautiful and healthy looking and you're glowing. What happened to all of you?"

Co-Co explained, "You're glowing too Runt. We told you; we're in Heaven and everything in Heaven is brand new. Everything here stays brand new forever."

I looked at my paws and legs and I was glowing too.

"Come on Runt, let's play," Co-Co said, and then barked.

As I looked around I was spellbound by what I saw. The beautiful field went on as far as I could see. There were huge trees and beautiful flowers everywhere, and a huge pond and everything looked bright and brand new. The pond sparkled and the water looked so clear, I could see all the way to the bottom. I looked up at the sky and there were cloud formations tinted with pink, blue, and gold. There was light, but no sun that I could see. This place was very strange and beautiful and I was happy, and for once in my life I felt safe.

"I'm in Heaven? What's that?" I asked as I looked around.

They all laughed again and Co-Co said, "You're dead and this is where you come when you die."

"I'm dead?" I asked incredulously, and then I remembered I was thrown in the air and hit something hard, and everything went dark.

Charlie said, "Don't be scared Runt, nothing here can ever hurt you. There is no sorrow, no pain, and no humans will hurt you here either. Every creature here loves you and everyone loves each other. Even the humans love us. We never have to leave and we're here forever."

"Where's Mom and all our other brothers and sisters?"

Dad said, "Don't worry Runt they'll be along soon enough."

Dad had been watching us quietly with loving eyes. His eyes were big and I knew he was happy.

"Am I dreaming?" I wondered out loud.

Co-Co said, "No Runt, this isn't a dream, come and play with us."

"Do I get to stay here with you guys?" I asked excitedly.

"We don't know you'll have to talk to Jesus. He's the one in charge here," Co-Co replied with a smile. "Let's play while there's time."

"What's a Jesus? Is he a human? I don't like humans."

"Don't worry about that right now. Jesus will be here soon to talk to you, but we can play until He comes. He is nice to us and He loves us."

Dad looked at me and said, "Everything will be fine Runt. This is the spirit world. God is a spirit, and this is the place he created for all spirits. There are only souls here in Heaven. Go play with your brother and sister, they're waiting for you."

"But I don't understand."

Charlie and Co-Co took off running and I followed them and then suddenly, they flew up into the blue sky and began to fly around like birds. "How did you do that?" I asked looking up at them, while they soared above me.

Charlie said, "Just think about it and you can do it. This place is great because you can do anything that you can think of."

I ran after them and I thought about flying and all of sudden, I was flying in the air with them! I was having such a great time and then I saw those crazy pigs and I got scared. Charlie said, "You don't have to be afraid of the pigs anymore Runt, they love us. I told you, everyone here loves each other."

One of the pigs flew over to me and said, "Howdy Runt!"

I was shocked and the pig laughed and flew away saying, "See ya later Runt, great to see you again."

I saw all kinds of birds, but many of them were walking around down below me and I asked Charlie why the birds were not flying like us. Charlie replied, "They said that they had always flown when they were alive on earth, and that they were just plumb tired of flying, and preferred to walk."

I asked Co-Co, "How long did you say we get to stay here?"

She smiled and said, "Forever."

"How long is forever?"

"Forever never ends."

"Never?"

"Never," she stated without hesitation.

"So, do I get to stay here forever too?"

"I can't tell you anything, you'll have to talk to Jesus about that."

We played for a long time just like we did when we were puppies on the farm. I was having such a wonderful time that I had forgotten about all the bad things that had ever happened to me. We flew around for a while and then we swam in the clear sparkling pond and we could breathe and talk under water. Eventually, we came out of the water and our fur was glowing even more than before. I was finally happy for once in my life and I wished with all my heart that Old Blue was here.

We ran through the fields chasing each other and sniffing the flowers, which seemed to give me energy. I rolled over on my back and looked up at the golden colored clouds, and I barked. This was the greatest place ever!

Suddenly, a brilliant white light appeared in the distant field. All the animals stopped playing and gathered around. They all began to jump excitedly looking in the direction of the light.

"What is it? I asked.

Charlie said reverently, "It's Jesus! He's coming to visit with us and I think he wants to talk with you."

"Talk to me about what? Did I do something wrong?" I asked worriedly. I wondered if he was going to hit me, or make me leave. I wanted to stay in this beautiful place with my family more than anything.

"No silly, Jesus always comes to meet the new arrivals to welcome them."

"Oh," I said, wondering what this Jesus wanted to talk to me about. I was apprehensive watching him as he approached. He was the most beautiful human I had ever seen and He was mesmerizing. I began to feel sad because I knew this Jesus would get rid of me too, like everyone else had.

When Jesus came closer, all the animals ran over to him. They were all jumping up and licking him, and he was laughing and petting them. I stood back away from everyone because I was scared that I would have to leave, and I loved it here. I thought maybe this Jesus guy would forget about me and leave me alone. I didn't want to leave and I didn't want to see any humans. After a few moments, Jesus told all the animals to go play and he promised that he would come back later to play with them. He looked over at me and walked over to where I was and said, "Hello little fellow, how are you?"

I didn't say anything, I just stared at him. I sniffed him, but he didn't smell like any human that I had ever smelled. Most humans stink, but he smelled like the flowers that grew in Farmer Sam's field. It was a sweet scent and it made me feel good.

"You're not going to talk to me?" He tilted his head to the side, and looked at me with a serious look.

"I don't like humans," I stated firmly.

He threw his head back and laughed.

"Why are you laughing at me?"

"Because I love you."

"You do?" I asked perplexed. "I thought all humans hated me... or, I mean hated animals."

"Not all humans hate animals. I love animals. Can I tell you a secret?"

"Yes," I said.

"I'm not a human," and he laughed again.

"You look like a human, but you don't smell like one."

Jesus laughed and his eyes sparkled.

"*Who* are you?" I asked.

80

"I am Jesus and I am the one who created you." He then looked at me with a serious look as though he was scrutinizing me.

"Created me? What does that mean?"

"It means I made you. I made your teeth that you bite humans with." Jesus said laughing.

"I only bit them because they were trying to hurt me," I said defensively.

"It's alright, that's why I gave you teeth. I made your legs, your head, and everything about you."

"You did?" I asked incredulously.

Jesus slowly nodded his head and said, "Yes, and I'm the one that put a spirit in you."

"A spirit?"

"Yes, that's what makes you…you."

"I heard you own this place," I said.

Jesus threw his head back and laughed uncontrollably.

It suddenly dawned on me that we were talking and understanding each other, just like I had with my Dad and my siblings. I asked him how it was possible that I could talk to a human and he said, "Your brother and sister already told you, you're in Heaven and you can do anything here. That's how we all talk here; with our thoughts."

81

I was suddenly happy and I decided I liked this human, or whatever he was. I couldn't be sure what he was, but I knew that he was different from any other human I had ever met. He looked human, but nothing about him was human. I could feel immense love radiating from him and I wasn't scared anymore. I asked him, "Can I stay here forever too, like the other animals? I want to stay here with my family, and I promise I'll be good, and not bite anyone."

Jesus looked at me and said, "I wanted to talk to you about that."

My happiness began to wane, because I knew that he was going to make me leave like all the other humans always did. I dropped my head and started to cry.

"Don't cry Buddy. I want to make a deal with you."

I looked up and asked what he wanted, but I had already decided that I wasn't going to do anything for him, unless he let me stay.

"I need you to go back and do something for me. It's very important to me."

"I don't want to go back. I want to stay here, please," I begged.

"I picked you because you're special."

"You think I'm special?" I asked in wonder. "Why?"

"Oh yes! I think you're very special and only you can do this task for me. There is a certain man that I want you to help, and no one else can do it. It means a lot to me and that makes you special."

82

"I really want to stay here." I begged.

"I'll make you a promise. If you go back and do this for me, I will bring you back here when you're finished, and you can live here forever. I will also give you more rewards than all the rest of the animals and I will make you the boss over all the dogs in Heaven."

"Really?"

"I promise," he said with all seriousness.

"Well...I don't know."

Jesus laughed again and said, "I'll even answer one request that you ask of me, and I'll make it come true."

I thought about it for a second and I thought to myself; I got him on this one. I said, "Ok, my request is… that I can stay here!"

Jesus laughed so hard I thought he was going to fall down.

"I think maybe I made you a little *too* smart." Then Jesus said, "Anything except that."

I thought for a moment, and then I knew what I wanted and I said, "I know! Can you bring Old Blue here?"

"No, it isn't his time yet. He has a job to do too."

"Well then...could you find him a good home? He's my best friend and he's old, and no humans want an old dog; could you give him a nice human and a good home in his old age?"

"Yes, I can do that. That is a great request and I knew you would not ask for yourself, but for someone else. You really are special."

"Who is this human I have to help, and why?"

"You will know in your spirit. It's time for you to go back now. Someone is praying for your return as we speak."

Suddenly, I woke up and I felt intense pain, and I saw a woman next to me and she had her hands on me. I thought it was Doctor Vickie, and I thought that I was having another dream. Then I saw Doctor Toby across the room and then the room began to spin around and everything went dark again.

## Chapter Eleven

# The Return Of Buddy

*V*ickie yelled, "Come quick Toby! The dog has come back to life! He's alive!"

Toby ran to the clinic and when he entered the room he stopped and stared at the dog. He couldn't believe his eyes, the dog *was* alive. The dog had died, and there was no mistake about it because he had been there when the dog had passed.

"How can he be alive?" Toby asked in wonderment. "It's impossible."

The dog was looking at him and then the dog whimpered and closed its eyes.

"It was my prayers," Vickie stated without hesitation.

"No, it had to be the defibrillator, or maybe the CPR. It just took a while to take effect, that's all," Toby said doubting his own words.

"Face it Toby, it was a miracle," Vickie said firmly. "You just can't admit that there is something out there that is more powerful than you, can you?"

Toby was not much of a believer, but this was hard to explain and it was more than he was able to comprehend. How did this dog come back to life? It was impossible and yet, he just couldn't bring himself to agree with Vickie's beliefs.

"It was just a lucky coincidence that's all," he said half heartedly.

"I thought you said you would be a believer if the dog came back to life," she said looking at him with her arms crossed. "And the dog is alive."

"Well, I have to admit it is a little strange," he said sheepishly.

She wasn't going to let him off the hook so easily and she said, "Can't you just accept that it was a miracle from God."

"I'm sorry honey, I concede and I apologize," he said sincerely.

"Are you serious, or are you just trying to make me happy?"

He looked at her and admitted, "I can't explain it, except to say that it was a miracle." Toby had to admit that there was nothing else to explain it because deep down in his heart, he knew it wasn't anything that they had done medically.

Toby and Vickie worked on the dog putting five stitches in the dog's head and four in his left side. Along with that, he had a concussion and three broken ribs and his left back leg was swollen. The dog had a damaged eye and Toby disinfected it with ointment and put a patch over the eye, claiming that the dog would never see out of it again. The dog had lost a lot of blood which alone should have killed him, and he had several bad bruises to his body. Over the next several weeks, the little dog was recovering at a speed that Toby could not believe. He thought to himself that maybe it was a miracle from God. He knew his wife believed completely in the Lord and maybe, just maybe; it *was* a true miracle. Later the dog regained the sight in his damaged eye and Toby was amazed, and he had to admit, that was a miracle in itself too.

Over the following days, everyone in the clinic knew about the miracle dog and had come to gaze at him in wonder.

When I woke up I was in a lot of pain and my thinking was not very clear. I couldn't see out of one of my eyes because something was covering it. My head was hurting so bad, that when I tried to move I passed out again.

Later when I woke up, there were a lot of humans coming into my room and staring at me. They came and went, and some of them petted me on my side, which I could do nothing about. I figured that one of them would take me away and hurt me some more, but I was too weak to care. Then I remembered the crazy dream I had that seemed so real. For a moment, I thought that maybe I had been in a real place, but then I thought no; it was just a stupid dream and I fell asleep.

*Chapter Twelve*

# The Execution Of Old Blue

O n the fourth day after waking up, I was feeling much better. I knew that I was right back in the place I had escaped from because I recognized the humans that were coming in and out of the clinic. I was back in jail and I was depressed knowing that I had done all that traveling, only to wind up right back where I started. Well, at least I would get to see Old Blue again and that made me happy. Wait till I tell him about my crazy dream. Won't he get a good laugh!

In the middle of the day, Dave brought Old Blue into the clinic followed by Doctor Toby and Doctor Vickie where Buddy was recovering. They placed Old Blue onto a table across the small room from Buddy.

I said, "Hey Blue!"

"How you doing kid. What are you doing here? I thought you'd be long gone by now."

"I don't know what happened because I don't remember too much."

"Say, you don't look so good, are you alright?"

"Yes. I'm ok, but I hurt a lot. Hey Blue, I had a crazy dream about you."

"Tell me about it kid. I'd love to hear all about it."

"I dreamed I went to a place called Heaven and there was this really beautiful bridge, and a huge field to play in. I saw my Dad, my brother, and my sister, and we played for a while, and then a human showed up; or…well I'm not sure what he was, but everyone called him Jesus. He told me that he created all of us and he wore a white robe."

Blue chuckled and said, "Gee kid, sounds like a real good dream. Go on, tell me more about this dream you had."

"Jesus said I had to go back and help a special human and he said that if I did, he would do one thing for me, and I told him that I wanted him to find you a good home."

"I wish it were true kid, but I'm afraid that most dreams don't come true for us," he said.

Dave was not in a good mood, and Doctor Toby asked him what was bothering him and Dave said, "I guess I'm just sad about Blue."

"Do you want me to do this? You can leave and I'll understand. I'll put him down if you want to leave."

"No, I want to be the one to do it. Blue trusts me and it'll be easier for him. It's just that…," he looked over at Buddy and said, "If it weren't for the money we had to spend to help that little dog over there," pointing at me, "There would be enough money to keep Blue alive a few more weeks and maybe he'd have a chance at a good home to spend his golden years in comfort."

"What's he talking about Blue?"

"Don't worry about it kid."

"Tell me Blue, what are they going to do to you?"

Blue sighed and answered in a low growl, "They have to put me down kid."

I asked choking back my tears, "You mean they are going to make you dead because of me?" I was scared. What if my dream wasn't true? Blue would be dead and it would be my fault.

"It's not your fault kid, don't blame yourself."

"No, they can't do that. This is my entire fault, it's not right."

"It's ok kid, I don't mind."

I started to struggle trying to get up, but I hurt too bad. "I'll help you Blue. I'll bite all of them and save you."

"Settle down kid before they stick you with a needle too. I want to go out with my dignity. I don't want these humans to think they broke my spirit."

Vickie, Dave, and Doctor Toby were watching the two dogs. The young one was trying to get up. Vickie said, "I think they know what's going on. That little one got upset when you two started talking about putting Blue down, and they look like they're talking to each other."

"Don't be ridiculous Vickie, they don't know what's going on," Toby said.

"Look at them! I swear that they're talking to each other," exclaimed Vickie.

They looked at both of the dogs and the little one was growling and whining, struggling to get up. Blue was looking over at the little dog, and he was whining and growling softly, opening his mouth, as though he were talking to the little dog.

Doctor Vickie went over to Buddy to try and calm him down, so he wouldn't tear his stitches.

"By gosh I think you're right Doctor Vickie," Dave said.

"You're both being ridiculous. Come on Vickie we need to finish that paperwork if we want those funds, let's leave Dave alone. It's hard enough on Dave without us making things worse." Toby said.

They left the room leaving Dave there by himself with the two dogs. Dave watched the dogs and wondered what they were saying to each other. The dogs had seemed to settle down now.

"I'm so sorry Blue. If I hadn't escaped, you would not have to be dead. It's all my fault; I wish they would make me dead instead of you. It isn't fair, I'm so sorry Blue."

"It'll be alright kid it's time for me to go. I've had a good life. It was a good dream you had kid, but it was just a dream. I guess this is good-bye. Take care of yourself kid and I hope you find a good human and a nice home." Old Blue chuckled and said, "Hey who knows? Maybe I'll go to that place you dreamed about."

Dave had taken the needle out and filled it with the deadly liquid. He turned the needle up towards the ceiling and tapped the air out with his finger. He turned to Blue and sighed heavily looking down at Blue and he said, "It'll be quick my old friend."

"No Blue...Noooo..." Buddy cried.

Dave stuck the needle into Blue's neck.

## Chapter Thirteen

# The Old Man

An old man pulled into the shelter parking lot and got out of his Cadillac. His name was George and he was seventy-five years old. His wife had passed on and he had no family to speak of. George was looking for a dog, and he wanted a dog that was old like him. He had recently lost his dog of fifteen years, and he was lonely. He loved dogs and he'd had a dog as a companion most all of his life. He was a stern no nonsense man and was always direct and to the point with everybody. He didn't care much for people, but he loved dogs.

He entered the shelter and walked over to the desk. His cobalt blue eyes looking over his glasses at the young girl sitting behind the counter and he asked, "Who's in charge around here?"

Heather the young office assistant looked up and asked, "Can I help you sir?"

"Why, yes you can young lady. I'm looking for an old dog. Not a young one mind you, but an old one like me. I figure if I adopt an old dog then maybe we'll both die together at about the same time. People don't care much for us old people; or old dogs either." He gave Heather a hard stare and said, "I don't want a young dog mind you, because he'll out live me, and then who do you think is going to take care of him young lady, you? And don't try to talk me into taking a young dog either. I'm old, but I'm not stupid. And if you can find me an old dog, I'll donate a hefty sum to the shelter. Please don't waste my time young lady."

"Yes sir. I understand," Heather thought this old man was strange and she was considering calling Doctor Vickie to deal with the old codger when she thought of Old Blue. Why he'd be perfect! Carmen had just walked up to the front desk and Heather turned and asked her, "Can you take this gentleman back to the kennel to look at Blue? He's interested in adopting an old dog and I thought Blue would be perfect for him."

Carmen exclaimed, "What? Oh my gosh!" She knew that Dave had taken Blue back to the clinic only a few minutes ago to euthanize him. She quickly turned and ran down the short hall praying she was not too late. Bursting through the door she yelled, "Stop Dave, Stop!" putting her hand out, palm straight up like a traffic cop.

Dave had just stuck the needle into Blue's neck when Carmen burst into the room and it scared him so bad, he jerked the needle out and said angrily, "You're not supposed to be in here. You almost scared me to death and you've upset Old Blue. This is a somber moment for me and this dog. What's wrong with you?"

"Dave, there's an old man out front that says he wants an old dog. We've found a home for Old Blue"

"What? Is this some kind of joke?" Dave asked. "If this is a joke, I swear..."

"Come out and see for yourself if you don't believe me," Carmen begged.

"Alright, I'm coming. This had better not be some kind of joke." Dave said angrily.

Dave left the room and I asked Blue what was going on and he said he wasn't sure, because humans were funny creatures. A couple minutes later, Dave and Carmen came back in the room with a brand new collar and leash. Dave told Blue that a man had come to adopt him and that he was going to a good home to live out his days in peace.

Dave put the collar and leash on him and just before Blue went out the door, he turned and said, "Hey kid, I guess that dream of yours was real. So long kid, I hope you find yourself a good home too."

I said, "Good luck Blue, I'll see you in that place called Heaven."

Blue laughed and said, "Yea kid, I'll see you in Heaven." Although Blue didn't believe in that stuff, he figured he'd still humor the poor kid.

Dave and Carmen saw Blue turn and give a short bark to the little dog and the little dog barked back twice at Old Blue. Dave and Carmen looked at each other with surprised looks and Dave said, "No, there's no way that just happened."

Doctor Toby was walking past when he heard Dave's comment, "Are you alright Dave?"

"I'm more than alright Doc," he said walking down the hall whistling, with Blue right behind him.

"What the…?" Doctor Toby said. "What's with him and what's he doing with Blue? I thought he was putting Blue down. What's going on around here?"

Carmen told Toby what had just happened and the Doctor was speechless.

Carmen also told him that the old man had donated five-thousand dollars to the shelter.

"It's another miracle Doctor Toby!" she said as she went down the hall smiling.

Doctor Toby's brow furrowed and he said, "I think I'll be going to Church with Vickie this Sunday."

## Chapter Fourteen
# Here We Go Again

*J*oe was a truck diver and his wife Sondra was home by herself most of the time, and she nagged him constantly saying, "I want a little house dog that can keep me company and warn me of any intruders while you're gone. If you really loved me, you'd get me a little house dog."

Today was Sondra's birthday and Joe had decided to get her a dog to keep her company and it would also shut her up...for a while anyway. He knew there was a shelter off the old highway if he could only find it. He went past the turn, seeing the sign just as he passed the entrance. Muttering under his breath, he found a graveled area on the side of the road where he could pull off and turn around. He then headed back up the highway towards the shelter.

Joe was forty years old and Sondra was three years younger than him. He and Sondra were not able to have children and he felt bad knowing that she had always wanted a child. He remembered how disappointed she was when they found out that she was unable to have a child. In a way, he was glad because he didn't like children; or animals. "I hope she appreciates this," he thought to himself as he drove.

He spotted the shelter and drove into the parking lot and turned off the ignition. He got out of the car and closed the door. He had bought a fancy purple collar and matching leash, which was Sondra's favorite color. He hoped it would fit the dog he picked out. He didn't know a lot about dogs because he had never owned an animal before and this was all new to him. Joe had never really cared much for animals because he thought they were dirty and nothing but a nuisance. However, he figured a dog was less expensive, and a lot less trouble than a child. Joe thought to himself, "I hope the dog I get is housebroken. I'll have to ask and make sure. I can't have an animal dirtying up my house because I work too hard for what I have." Joe loved his car too, almost as much as he loved Sondra. Joe's car was garage kept and he washed and waxed the car on a regular basis. The thought of putting a dirty animal in his car made him cringe, but for Sondra, he would do it just this once. He had laid an old patched quilt down across the back seat to keep the dog from getting the seat dirty and shedding all over his back seat.

When he entered the shelter he could smell the animals and wondered if he should get a dog, because it might make his house smell like this place. He went up to the desk and said, "I'm looking for a small dog for my wife. She really wants one and it's her birthday today and I thought I would surprise her with a dog."

Heather smiled and said, "One moment, and I'll have someone take you through the kennel and you can look at the dogs."

"Great," he responded as he looked around the room.

Heather called Carmen and told her the gentleman at the desk would like to look at the dogs. Carmen took Joe into the kennel and she stood at the door in case Joe had any questions. Joe slowly walked down the line of cages looking at the dogs. He said more to himself than to Carmen, "That one's too big; that one too, and that one's too old. I want a younger one; but not too young." He stopped at Buddy's cage and looked at him. "He's kinda cute. What's his name?"

While Buddy was under sedation, Dave had trimmed his hair and bathed him. Buddy looked very presentable and had healed nicely. Dave had made the comment, that the little dog was really cute, once he was cleaned up.

"He doesn't have a name. We just call him Squirt here at the shelter."

"That's great; my wife would love to name him herself. Is he housebroken?"

"Well...I can't say for sure. I would think he is, because we never have to clean his waste up in his cage and he always goes when we take him for a walk."

Joe stood there and considered it for a few moments looking at the dog. The dog just stared at him.

I saw the man looking at me and I wondered if this was the person I was supposed to help, but I sensed he didn't really like me. Was this the human I was supposed to help? The man in my dream must have been real because he saved Blue, so I thought maybe this man was the one. It had been four weeks since my dream and Doctor Vickie said that I had healed very quickly and they had placed me in Old Blue's cell. They had declared me ready for adoption.

"Alright, I'll take him."

"Great, go out to the main desk and Heather will draw up the paperwork. I'll put the collar and leash on him and bring him right out." Joe handed the collar and leash to Carmen and went out to the front desk.

I thought that I should be good since this might be the human that the man in the dream told me about. I let Carmen put the collar and leash on me and I followed her out to the front thinking, "Here we go again."

Joe put his wife's new dog in the back seat of the car and pointed at him saying, "Don't mess in my car little dog or you'll be sorry." Then Joe got into the car and drove home, looking back occasionally to make sure the dog wasn't doing anything it shouldn't be doing.

When he got home, he took the dog out of the back of the car and walked the dog to the front door and rang the doorbell. He heard his wife say, "Who is it?"

Joe said, "Special delivery." He heard his wife unlock the door and when she opened the door she looked at Joe first, and then down at the dog and squealed, "Oh Joe, you got me a little doggie! Oh Joe! Bring him in."

Joe said, "Happy Birthday Sondra."

"Oh Joe, he's so cute," she said in a little girl's high pitched voice.

"Take good care of him and he'll take good care of you," Joe said laughing.

"What's his name?"

"He doesn't have one, so you get the pleasure of naming him."

"Oh goody, let's see…how about…Baby! Yes, I like that name because he is going to be the little baby we never had."

Joe had some time off before he had to hit the road again and several weeks had passed and everything was going just fine, until Sondra decided to curl Baby's hair with a hot curling iron, and put pink ribbons in Baby's hair. Sondra filled a squirt bottle with water and sprayed the dog's long hair, holding the dog down on the couch because he kept squirming around. She had plugged the curling iron in and it had gotten hot enough to start the process. After making several curls, the dog bit her.

I didn't bite her too hard, just enough to make her stop burning me with that contraption that felt like fire against my skin. She yelled and screamed at me, and I ran and hid under the couch. The man named Joe came into the living room looking for me and he started yelling for me to come out, but I stayed under the couch and hoped that if I was quiet, he would go away; but he didn't.

"Come out of there you little heathen. I'm going to give you a whipping."

I don't think so pal. I believe I'll stay right here where you can't reach me and by the way, just a warning; I wouldn't stick my hands down here if I were you.

Joe went and got a bat saying, "I'll get him out of there or else."

"No, don't you dare Joe," Sondra warned. "That's my Baby."

Sondra had examined her hand and the bite wasn't so bad, although it did hurt a lot. There wasn't much blood, but it hurt to the bone. Joe was still mad and he said, "It's going to be a dead Baby when I get a hold of him, the little varmint. No animal bites my wife and gets away with it. I knew getting a dog was a bad idea. I thought there was something wrong with him, because all he does is sit and stare at you."

Joe was hoping something like this would happen, so that he could get rid of this nasty little animal. He got Sondra a dog and she couldn't say he didn't try. He had been a good husband and had gotten a dog like she wanted and now he had the perfect excuse to get rid of it. Sondra couldn't say he hadn't tried.

"Please don't hurt him Joe."

"Sondra, we can't have an animal that's going to bite you every time you touch him. He's got to go. He snapped at you once when you tried to give him a bath and now, he's bitten you. He's got to go. This dog is a biter and we can't have that."

Sondra started crying and pleading through her tears, "No, please Joe don't hurt him."

Joe hated when she cried and he relented saying, "Ok, I won't hurt him." He looked at her and said, "Let me see your hand."

She showed him her hand and she said, "It isn't so bad Joe and he didn't really mean to bite me."

"Oh, he didn't mean it huh? He just accidentally opened his mouth and closed it on your hand by mistake? No, he's got to go; he can't stay here. I knew this was a bad idea anyway."

"Please Joe, I want a dog. Just give him another chance."

"Sondra, I don't want to come home one night and find out that your face has been chewed off by this crazy dog."

Joe took a deep breath and calmed down and said in a normal tone hoping to talk some sense to Sondra, "I tell you what. I'll take him to the other side of town and let him loose and we'll look for another dog when I come back off the road again. This dog is no good because he's tainted. There's something wrong with him. He's not the dog for you."

Joe had no intentions of getting another dog, but told Sondra that just to make her happy. He wished now he had never gotten this dog. He knew that this had been a big mistake.

Sondra sniffed and said, "Ok Joe, but couldn't you take him back to the shelter where he'll be safe, instead of just kicking him out in the street? It's awful cold outside Joe."

"Now wouldn't I look stupid taking the dog back that I just got? Besides, they might charge me more money to take him back and if I take him back, they might put him to sleep if I tell them he bites. He'll have a fighting chance if I let him loose and somebody will probably find him and take him in. Then he'll be somebody else's problem."

"I suppose you're right," she agreed.

I saw that things had settled down and I thought that maybe the man wasn't mad at me anymore, so I came out from under the couch. The man came in the room and squatted down and talked nicely to me saying, "Come on boy, we're just going for a little ride." He put the collar and leash on me and took me outside to the car, placing me in the back seat. He got into the car, started the engine, and we left.

Joe turned his head around looking in the back seat at the dog and said, "I'm taking you to the mountain instead to make sure you don't find your way back. Sorry little doggie but you are a biter, and we can't have that. Maybe someone will find you and take you in, if you're lucky. But you're not going to be my problem anymore, you stupid little mutt. You're lucky I didn't hurt you. You can thank Sondra for that."

I didn't understand everything he said, but I understood enough to know that he didn't like me and he wanted me to leave. We drove for a while and then we stopped at the foot of a mountain. He got out of the car and took the collar and leash off of me. Then he took me out of the car and set me on the side of the road saying, "Good luck mutt." I stood there watching as he got back into the car and sped away into the cold, dark night.

That stupid human would find out later that I had marked his car, just before he pulled over to throw me out.

## Chapter Fifteen
# Back To The Woods

*I* looked up at the night sky. It was a clear moonless night, and there must have been a million stars stretching across the heavens. Across the road, was a large field and behind me, was a large valley. I turned towards the valley and I began searching for a safe place to sleep. I was cold and tired. I sniffed and searched around for a while and I found a recess in some rocks at the foot of one of the mountains about half way down the long valley. There was enough room for me to squeeze into the small crevice and once I entered the opening, I saw that it was a small den that went back a few feet. There was plenty of room, so I crawled to the back of the burrow and curled up. I heard a scream in the distance and I knew it came from one of those big cats that Mama had warned me to stay away from. She told me that they were like those crazy pigs on the farm and they would eat me.

As I lay there, I thought back about Claire and the warm little house where I had stayed for awhile, and it seemed so long ago. I could almost feel the warmth from the heater, and that had been my favorite place to sleep at night. I wished that I was there right now. Claire wasn't so bad and she never really bothered me and perhaps, if the house hadn't caught on fire, I would still be there. I was beginning to think that I would never find the farm and I had just about given up on ever finding it. I missed my family and I was lost.

I started crying and wondered why nobody loved me. It seemed like nothing ever worked out for me. Why couldn't I be as lucky as Old Blue? I was glad that he had found a home and I thought that maybe someday I would find a good home too; but I wasn't counting on it. Maybe I should just go outside and let that big cat eat me. I wouldn't ever have to worry about anything ever again and I could go to Heaven and be with my family. I wondered again if the strange dream that I had was real and I wished I could be back there in that place called Heaven with my family. Maybe if I went to sleep, I would go there again and so, I fell asleep dreaming of that place called Heaven.

The following morning, I woke up and peeked out of the mouth of my small cave. It was so foggy I couldn' t see anything at all, but by noon the fog had lifted somewhat, and it had begun to rain.

I came out of my hole and looked down towards the end of the valley. I saw two houses and I decided to walk to the first house and see if I could find something to eat. When I finally reached the first house, I saw a small building just off to the left side of the big house. I stopped behind the little building, peeking around the corner. I watched the house, lingering for several minutes to make sure no humans were around. I saw a black bag at the end of the house and I decided to chance investigating the bag. I saw no human movement, so I went up to the bag and sniffed it and I smelled food.

I grabbed the bag with my teeth and shook my head back and forth until the bag ripped. I found a small amount of food and I ate what was there. I was still hungry, so I headed towards the second house. Once I got near the second house, I stopped and looked around for a minute or two. Seeing no one, I started sniffing the air. I smelled food, and I followed the smell. It was beginning to rain a little harder as I spotted two bags by the back of the house. I ripped one open and there was nothing in it, so I tore the other one open. I found a small amount of food and I ate it all and I was still hungry, but I was satisfied. The rain had begun to beat down harder and it was very cold, so I decided to retreat back to my small lair.

I stopped at the pond and lapped up some water and after doing my business I returned to my hiding place and went to sleep. I stayed in my cave the rest of the day and most of the next, except to go get a drink from the pond several times. When night fell, I began to ponder my situation and I knew that sooner or later, I would have to leave this place in order to find something to eat. I was tired and although I was cold, I fell asleep immediately.

In the morning, I crawled to the mouth of the hole and peeked out to make sure there was no danger waiting for me. I crawled out into the bright sunshine and it was still very cold outside, but the sun was bright and warm. I scouted around for something to eat, but everything was dead and bare. I thought that maybe I could find some apples, but there was nothing. I went over to the pond and took a deep long drink, and then I went over to a leafless tree and did my business. I continued to look around for a while thinking that I might find some food, but there was none to be had. I knew that big cat was out there somewhere, probably looking for me and I had to be careful. I decided to get another drink and then I would leave this valley and continue my search for the farm.

Carl and Tommy were walking along the side of the mountain just above Big John's property. It was Saturday and Carl's mother was at work and his father had gone into town to play cards. Carl had snuck his father's rifle out of the house and they were looking for something to shoot at. As they were walking along the side of the mountain, Carl spotted a little dog down along the foot of the mountain on Big John's property. The dog was at the edge of the pond drinking water.

"Hey look Tommy there's a dog down by the pond. Let me see if I can hit him."

As Carl looked through the scope Tommy said, "No Carl, don't shoot that little dog. That's Big John's property and if he sees us shooting onto his property, we'll be in big trouble."

"I ain't worried about Big John and besides, he won't know if you don't tell him. Now stop acting like a little wimp."

"You shouldn't shoot that poor little dog Carl. That's wrong and besides; that could be John's dog, and then we'll really be in trouble."

Carl looked through the scope, aimed, and pulled the trigger. The rifle cracked and jumped in Carl's hands and Carl yelled, "I got him." The two boys watched as the dog rolled over on the ground, got up, and took off running, disappearing behind a pile of boulders.

"I hit him, I know I did!" Carl exclaimed. "Let's go see where he went and finish him off."

"Are you crazy? I'm not going down there on Big John's property. I'm getting outta here. You probably killed that poor little dog."

"You sissy," Carl said in disgust.

"I can't believe you shot that poor little dog! You probably killed him," Tommy said, with tears in his eyes.

Tommy was scared now and wished he had never come out here with Carl. He turned and left in the direction of his house and Carl followed him, calling him a sissy boy.

All of a sudden, I felt a burn across the middle of my back and I heard a loud crack. It knocked me over and I rolled on the ground. Quickly getting up, I ran as fast as I could to my hole, wondering what had happened. The middle of my back felt like it was on fire and I could feel warm liquid seeping down the side of my body. I got into my hole and decided to stay hidden for the rest of the day.

After several hours, my back still burned and it had become stiff, especially after laying still for a while. I could still feel the warm liquid seeping down my side once in a while, but mostly when I moved around. I snuck out once to drink from the pond at dusk, but quickly retreated back to my hole. I had decided to leave the valley in the morning when I woke up and continue my search for the farm. The night was cold and I was in pain. I cried myself to sleep having no dreams; because I had nothing to dream about anymore.

The next morning I woke up to a strange sound at the opening of my hiding place. I couldn't place it right away and then as I woke up and my eyes focused, I knew what it was. It was that cat and he was clawing at the rocks and dirt trying to get to me. I was scared and I didn't know what to do, except to scrunch back in my hiding place as far as I could get.

The big cat had smelled blood and had traced it to this small hole. The cat knew there was something wounded hiding in the hole and the cat was hungry. He knew that whatever was in the hole would make a good breakfast. He began to claw the dirt and rocks away to make the hole big enough to reach in and snag whatever was in there with his sharp claws. He hadn't eaten in three days and food was scarce. The smell of blood made his mouth water with hunger.

Suddenly, I heard a loud thump and the cat turned and barred his teeth at something that was outside and then it ran away. Not long after that, I heard human voices and they were coming towards me. I lay very quiet hoping they would go past my hiding place, because I knew that they were probably as dangerous as the big cat.

Then I saw a man with a bunch of red fur on his face looking in the opening of my hiding place. He was shining a bright light at me and I knew I had been discovered. I gave a warning growl and I backed up as far as I could. There were two of them and I could hear them talking to each other. Then I saw a big human hand coming into the hole towards me. I bit the hand, but it wasn't a good bite. However, it did make the man take his hand out. I barely nicked him. This human was very fast.

## Chapter Sixteen
# Big John Finds A Dog

*B*ig John was a big man, hence the name; Big John. He stood
at six feet, three inches and tipped the scales at almost three
hundred pounds. On his head he wore a black cowboy hat that
was in contrast to his bushy red beard. Circling around the top of
his faded blue jeans was a wide, brown leather belt that sported a
large, oval-shaped silver horse-head buckle, and his favorite green
flannel shirt was tucked into his jeans. On his feet, were a pair of
brown cowboy boots that were worn and scuffed from much use,
and as far as anyone knew; they were the only pair of footwear
he'd ever owned.

Big John was fifty-three years old and he had been married for
nearly twenty years to his wife Donna, and one day she surprised
John by asking him for a divorce. Six months ago, she had moved
to the city for what she described as, "the finer life" leaving Big

John by himself, with the exception of an old hound dog named Duke who was John's favorite companion. Duke went everywhere John went and John loved him with all his heart. Then Duke died a month after Donna had left and it crushed Big John; but he would never allow anyone to see his pain.

Big John lived on a small family farm that he had inherited from his father, which had been handed down through the generations. The farm was situated at the end of a large valley which John owned. The farm was a small outfit, but he lived comfortably and Big John loved it. The farm house he lived in was a medium sized rancher and it was nothing fancy, but John was happy living there.

Ed Sheehan was Big John's best friend and his farm bordered John's property. They had known each other for many years, and Ed and John were as close as brothers, or as Ed liked to think; father and son.

Ed was seventy-two years old and he was as healthy as an eighteen year old. His face was tanned and weather worn and his grey goatee was short and trimmed. His favorite winter attire was a black knit stocking cap, tan colored bib overhauls, and dark brown combat boots. Hanging out of his right back pocket was a red bandana, decorated with long curly white designs; which was mostly for show.

When Ed finished his breakfast, he shrugged on his coat and backpack, and then he left the house. He began walking towards Big John's place which was less than a quarter mile to the east. He could have driven his old truck, but he liked to walk. There was a pink hue in the cold morning sky that was fading fast, as the sun began to rise from behind the mountain. Ed looked towards John's house in the distance and saw smoke rising from the chimney. The smoke seemed to slowly drift upward in the cold air, creating a grey-white haze in the morning sky far above the roof of the house. In the meadow, the brown, dead grass was covered with thick frost and the bright morning sunlight gave the illusion that the pasture was scattered with thousands of diamonds; each one sparkling. The morning air was very cold and with every breath Ed took, it formed a long vapor trail as he exhaled. Ed loved to walk and he loved the outdoors.

When he arrived at John's house he knocked on the door. He heard Big John holler, "Come on in Ed." Ed turned the knob, pushed the door open, and entered the warm living room. Big John was at the sink washing the morning dishes and at the far end of the room, Ed noticed that John had just recently stoked the fireplace and the flames were blazing. The heat felt good and the warmth from the fire began to slowly lessen the chill Ed felt from the walk over to John's house.

John asked, "Want something to eat?"

"No. Joanne made me breakfast this morning, but thanks anyway, and 'sides, you're cooking ain't all that."

John turned and grimaced at Ed.

"Did you find that cow yet?" Ed asked.

"No, I think I'm gonna look in the south end of the valley this morning. I reckon she's there."

Ed said, "More than likely, we've looked everywhere else. I seen the tracks of a big cat around, you might want to find that cow today and get her closer to home." Then Ed asked, "You have any raccoons visit you lately? Something was into my trash the other day and whatever it was, it scattered garbage everywhere."

"Yeah, they visited me too and I had to pick up trash first thing this morning."

John finished up the dishes, dried his hands on a dirty towel, and shrugged his coat on saying, "You ready old man?"

"Old man! Huh, I can dance circles around you."

Big John chuckled and walked out the door, with Ed following behind.

John turned and said, "Well old man, let's get to dancing."

They walked towards the mountains and into the long, wide valley.

After walking in silence for a ways, Ed hesitantly asked, "So… you doing alright?"

John looked over at Ed and asked, "What are you talking about?"

"You know, with Donna and Duke, and all that?"

"Yeah Ed, that's been a while." After a short pause John confided, "You know, Duke's passing hurt more than Donna leaving me. I miss that old boy."

Ed smiled and said, "Well, Joanne made me ask. She's worried about you."

"Well, you can tell her to stop worrying."

They continued walking without speaking for some distance. After searching for some time, they still hadn't located the cow and they decided to take a break half way up the valley, near the foot of the mountain. Ed pulled out his pipe and a bag of tobacco from his pocket. He began to stuff the pipe with the brown shredded tobacco and after he had filled the pipe to the top, he packed it down with his thumb. Then he pulled out a wooden kitchen match and struck the tip of the match on his pants leg. The match burst into an explosive flame and after the flame settled down, Ed put the flame up to the bowl of the pipe. Ed puffed and puffed until the pipe was thoroughly lit. John was looking at him smiling.

"Something funny?" Ed asked puffing on his pipe.

John chuckled and said, "It ain't the tobacco that's going to kill you Ed, it's all that huffing and puffing that's gonna to do you in."

Ed replied, "Ya think?"

Ed began to scan the valley, puffing his pipe thoughtfully. His green eyes reflected years of knowledge and experience, and he knew every inch of the canyon. Suddenly Ed said, "Well looky there John." Ed was pointing towards a big pile of rocks about five hundred yards to the left, towards the middle of the valley, up against the mountain and just below the bare tree line.

John looked over at Ed and asked, "What?" as he followed Ed's pointing finger. "Look at the foot of the mountain over by that pile of rocks yonder." Ed said

John saw a large mountain lion digging at a pile of big rocks up against the foot of the mountain and said, "He's after something. He's got some kinda critter holed up in there looking to eat for dinner."

"Yeah, wonder what it is?"

Big John carried a .357 magnum on his right hip and he pulled it out and handed it to Ed and as Ed took the gun he asked,

"John, what are you doing?" Big John didn't answer and he began walking towards the mountain lion, with Ed following behind. John scanned the ground and saw a thick branch about four feet long and he stopped and picked it up. He hefted it in his right hand and began to advance towards the lion. Ed whispered a warning, "Be careful John."

The big, yellow-brown cat was so busy trying to get into the hole that it didn't notice John and Ed, until they had come within fifty yards of it.

Finally, the big cat noticed them and it whipped around towards John baring its teeth, letting out an eerie scream as if to tell John this is my dinner, go away. John looked around and found a fist sized rock, and throwing the branch on the ground, he scooped up the rock with his right hand.

"Cover me Ed," John said softly. "Don't shoot him unless you got to."

"Gotcha covered Big John," Ed replied, aiming the pistol at the big cat. John slowly moved towards the big cat until he was within thirty yards of the animal. He took aim and threw the rock as hard as he could at the ground in front of the cat. The rock hit the ground right in front of the lion and bounced up, hitting the lion in the side near the cat's front leg. The lion bared his teeth and screamed once more, then turned and quickly disappeared into the underbrush. John stood there and watched the area where the lion had disappeared to make sure it didn't turn around and come back. He knew the lion wouldn't stray too far from his dinner ticket.

Ed walked up handing the pistol back to John saying, "Are you plumb crazy?"

John didn't reply as he took the weapon and holstered it. Then he continued walking towards the rocks to see what was there.

"Careful," Ed warned.

John approached the rocks with caution and as he drew closer, he spotted what appeared to be a small burrow back under the rocks. John squatted down and peered into the hole. The recess looked to be about four to five feet back in the rocks with a small opening, which perhaps a small animal could squeeze into. He could see where the mountain lion had been clawing at the ground trying to dig his way in to get whatever was in the small opening.

"Ed you got your flashlight on ya?"

"Yeah John, here you go," Ed handed John a long silver flashlight that shone a beam so powerful, that on a dark night it seemed to reach all the way to Heaven.

Ed whispered, "Be careful Big John it could be a skunk and if he sprays you, I won't be visiting you for quite some time."

"Shut up Ed, it's too late in the morning for a skunk," John said.

"I don't know John it's still kinda early yet."

John turned on the flashlight and peered into the hole carefully.

What John saw startled him and made him jump, because the animal growled when John turned the light on him. At first he couldn't tell what it was and then he realized that it was a small dog. The poor thing was shaking from the cold and it looked to be in miserable condition. The dog was so dirty and its hair was so long, it was almost unrecognizable.

"Well, what is it John?" Ed asked impatiently.

"Well, I'll be," John exclaimed.

"What is it?" Ed asked again more eagerly.

"Guess," John asked.

"A skunk?"

"No."

"A groundhog?"

"No."

"A wounded bird?"

"No."

"Dag nab it John! What is it?" Ed said exasperated.

"It's a dog Ed."

"A dog!? What's a dog doing way out here in a hole? Does he think he's a groundhog or something?" Ed looked down and exclaimed. "Look at that John." Ed pointed to the ground. "There's a few spots of blood leading into that hole. He's hurt. That's why that cat was after him. He smelled blood."

"We 'gotta get him out of this hole Ed. The poor thing is cold and scared." John reached into the hole and jerked his hand back quickly yelling, "He bit me!"

"Serves you right," Ed said with satisfaction. "That's what you get for playing guessing games with me. Too bad it wasn't a skunk." Then Ed relented asking, "Is it bad?"

"No," John replied. "I jerked my hand back before he could get a good hold on me." John looked at his hand and there was a spot of blood forming where the small nick was.

Ed asked, "How do you propose we get him out of that hole?"

John turned to Ed and said, "I got an idea."

"Same kinda idea you had just before you got your hand bit?" Ed asked with a grin on his face.

"Oh you're real funny old man," John said. "Here's what we'll do. Give me a piece of that jerky you carry and I'll put it in front of the hole. When he sticks his head out to take the jerky, I'll grab him by the scruff of the neck. You hold the backpack open and I'll stuff him down in it. Just make sure you hold the pack open for me so he don't bite me again. We gotta do this quick," John instructed.

Ed reached into his pocket and pulled out a plastic zip lock baggie full of jerky. He pulled a piece out and handed it to John. Big John took it and placed the strip of jerky in front of the hole.

John and Ed waited a couple of minutes when Ed grew impatient.

"Well John, he ain't 'gonna come out if you're right in front of the hole where he can see you."

I saw one of the men put a piece of meat in front of the opening of my little cave and I could smell it from where I was. I was hurt somewhat, but I was sure I could get the meat before they could hurt me. I was so hungry, that smelling that hunk of meat sitting in front of the hole was making me drool. I licked my lips and decided to take a chance.

John looked up at Ed and then moved off to the side, with his hand hovering over the top of the hole, out of the animal's sight and waited. After a short period of time, the dog quickly stuck his head out and grabbed the piece of jerky and disappeared back into the hole before John could grab him.

"What a great plan you came up with John." Ed hollered, laughing and slapping his knee. "Boy, this is great entertainment. I'm glad I tagged along this morning."

John ignored Ed and said, "I didn't think he was that fast. Give me another piece of jerky."

Ed handed John another piece of jerky and John set it in front of the hole again. "I'll get him this time."

"Sure you will John, or maybe he'll get you."

The dog's head popped out and snatched the second piece of jerky and returned back in the hole as quickly as he came out.

These humans were not only slow; they're stupid too. The meat was really delicious and I was starving! Maybe they'll pour some water in here too. I'm kind of thirsty and I could use a drink of water.

Ed couldn't help himself. He laughed and said, "Shucks John, why don't I just throw the whole bag in the hole and then we can just sit and wait 'till he comes out to use the bathroom. Then we can snatch him up while he's doing his business." Ed was laughing hysterically by this time.

John gave him an agitated look and said, 'Oh, you're so funny, you 'outa have your own TV show. Just give me another piece of meat Mr. Know It All."

Ed, still laughing stuck a piece of meat out at Big John and when John reached for it, Ed pulled it back laughing and said, "You better be quicker than that John. You want another piece of 'dog-gone' meat do ya? Get it...dog gone. Dog took meat...and dog gone." Ed doubled over laughing and John quickly snatched the piece of meat out of Ed's hand and placed the meat in front of the hole again.

Without looking up John said, "Shut up Ed." Several seconds later, the dog stuck his head out to grab the piece of meat and quick as lightening, John grabbed him by the neck and lifted him up, and out of the hole. "Gotcha," John exclaimed.

The little dog was growling and snarling and his legs were running in the air trying to find ground. John said, "Boy, he's mad as all get out! He sure is a handful for a little dog." And then John hollered, "Ed, get that backpack over here now."

"Ok, don't get your pants in a bunch." Ed replied laughing, as he opened the backpack. John dropped the little bedeviled dog into the pack, closed the flap, and fastened the strap down. The dog was barking and they could see the dog fighting trying to get out.

"There, now he can't get out," John said with satisfaction.

"Now what?" Ed asked.

"We'll take him back to my place where it's warm and get him something to eat. He should be warm in the backpack until we get back to the house," John said.

"You can carry the pack, I ain't getting bit," Ed said.

John and Ed started back towards the house and after a while, the dog quit fighting.

Ed stopped and said, "What about that stray cow John?"

"Oh yeah, I forgot."

Ed sighed and said, "Take the dog on back. I'll find the cow."

When the man grabbed me I tried to fight and get loose, but he shoved me into a bag. I was trapped again!

## Chapter Seventeen
# A Temporary Home

When John returned to his house he loosened the straps and laid the pack down on the floor to let the dog out and as the dog came out, he snapped at John. The little dog advanced toward John and barked, ready to fight. John could see the little dog was mad.

"Woah now, ain't you feisty. You're pretty tough for a little dog." John said amused. John admired the spunk of this little dog. The little dog just stared at him, ready to attack. "You're a mess. What happened to you, and how in the world did you get out here?" The dog continued to stare at him. John noticed that the dog was dirty and his hair was long and matted.

On closer inspection, John saw a bloody furrow across the dog's back. "Why by golly, I think you been shot. Looks like a bullet creased your back."

The fire had gone down and the house was chilly. John went over and built up the fire, throwing several logs in the fireplace. The small fire crackled, and sparks shot up the chimney. He went into the kitchen and opened the cabinet door and took out both of Duke's old plastic dog bowls. He turned the cold water spigot on and filled one bowl with water and placed it on the floor by the hearth. John had bought a bag of dog food just before Duke had passed and it was still in the closet. John had kept the bag of food in the pantry as though he was expecting Duke to come back someday. He then filled the other bowl with dry dog food and set it beside the water bowl. John looked at the dog and said, "There boy, help yourself."

John went into the spare bedroom and dug Duke's old bed out of the closet and set it by the fireplace. He paused looking at the dog, and then he went and sat down at the kitchen table watching the dog, wondering how he came to be in his valley.

The kitchen and living room were all one open space. The living room floor was hardwood and the only thing that separated the kitchen from the living room, was where the grey linoleum kitchen floor met the hardwood floor. The living room had a bay window and a fireplace. The fireplace was at the end of the room and just a few feet off to the left of the fireplace, set John's favorite easy chair. From his easy chair he could see the fireplace to his left and look straight out the bay window too. Just to the right of John's favorite chair there was a couch and a love seat. In front of the couch was a long wooden coffee table with a green tinted glass top.

As I ate, I watched the man and I knew that he was the one I saw peering into my hiding place. He was the one with the red fur on his face. The one I bit. I watched him carefully while he placed the bowls on the floor. I could smell the food and I was starving, but I waited until the man sat down and then I walked over to the food, sniffed it, and began to eat. I kept my eye on the man in case he tried to hurt me and as I chewed the food, I looked around for a place to run and hide if he tried to hurt me. I saw a couch across the room and I wondered if I could make it across the room and under the couch, before the man could catch me. I was so hungry and thirsty that I kept eating and hoping the man would not get up, but I was ready to run if I had to.

John watched as the dog went over to the bowl of food, sniffed it for a moment, and then began to eat. The dog only stopped eating long enough to take a drink of water; all the while keeping an eye on John. In a matter of minutes, the food and most of the water were gone and the dog was licking his lips and staring at John.

"You want more?" asked John. The dog just stared at him, so John filled the bowls with food and water again and the dog proceeded to eat all the dog food, and then he drank all the water. After emptying both bowls, the dog walked over to the fire and sat down facing John, just staring at him. The dog was so tired that he eventually lay down by the fire in Duke's old bed and fell asleep.

After I ate all the food and quenched my thirst, I went over and got into the soft bed and sat down. My belly was full and the heat from the fire began to penetrate my body and it made me so sleepy, that I had to lie down. Somewhere, I let my guard down and I fell asleep.

Later in the afternoon Ed came to John's house.

"Did you find that cow?" John asked.

"Yeah."

Ed pulled up a chair and sat down at the table with John. They sat at the kitchen table watching the dog sleep and discussing what to do about him. As they talked, Ed puffed on his pipe blowing smoke rings. He took a puff and blew a grey-blue smoke ring that wafted up towards the ceiling and slowly dissipated. They stared at the dog sleeping by the fire and kept their voices low, so as not to awake the poor animal.

"Ed, take a look at his back. Looks like a bullet crease across the middle there," John said.

Ed walked over quietly and took his pipe out of his mouth. He bent down and examined the dog's back and shook his head. "Someone's done shot this poor critter. Wonder who did that? Come to think of it, I thought I heard a gunshot the other day." Ed said with a disgusted look on his face. Shaking his head, he walked back over to the table and sat down.

"Looks like that wound could use a stitch or two John. It's still bleeding a little bit. Stitches might help it mend quicker. If not, it's liable to keep opening up and it might not stop bleeding."

"Yeah, that's going to be a little hard to do because he's already tried to bite me twice. He's a cocky little rascal and he ain't afraid of nothing," John said smiling. "You gotta admire him. He's pretty tuff for a little dog and it looks as though he's been through a lot."

When I woke up, the two humans that had brought me here were sitting at a table watching me. I hurt something awful and my back was stiff, and I was thirsty. I looked over at the bowls and saw that one was full of water and the other full of food. I went over to the bowls, not taking my eyes off the two men.

"Go ahead boy and get your fill. Nobody's going to hurt you," John said.

I drank some water and sat down, watching the two men.

"You gonna put an ad in the paper?" asked Ed watching the dog.

"For what?" John asked.

"Well, he's a lost dog and I'm sure someone's looking for him."

"A dog that's in the shape he's in? He doesn't even have a collar, or tags." John shook his head. "Nobody's looking for this dog Ed. You can tell he's been badly abused and I can tell he's a loner like me. You just keep quiet about the dog Ed." John warned.

"Yes sir. A loner just like you. Yep, two peas in a pod," Ed said smiling, his eyes twinkling, and then he added, "Don't you worry none John I won't say a word about your dog-napping ways."

"Very funny Ed," John said.

"Well, seeing how's you're gonna keep him, have you thought of a name yet?"

"Huh? Oh, no I haven't," John said with a sigh.

"How 'bout BJ?" Ed offered.

"BJ? Where did you come up with that name?" John asked.

"Why John, don't you know your own initials," Ed replied smugly.

"Oh yeah...BJ...hmmm...yeah, I like that. BJ it is. That's a great name, if I do say so myself," John said laughing. "Now I gotta figure out how I'm gonna stitch him up. I think there's some sleeping pills in the medicine cabinet that Donna used to take when she couldn't sleep. I'll use them and it will probably help his pain too."

Ed was looking at the dog when his eyes narrowed, as an idea formed in his head. He took his pipe out of his mouth and pointing the stem at BJ, he asked, "You know something John?"

"What's that?"

"I'll bet a dollar to a doughnut that BJ was the one that got into our garbage."

"It's possible I guess. No telling how long BJ was out there in the valley."

I knew that these two men called John and Ed were talking about me. So...they suspected me of stealing their trash. Well, they couldn't prove it was me. I'll just keep a straight face and they'll never know it was me. I continued to stare at them like I didn't know what they were talking about.

After Ed left, John crushed up some sleeping pills and an aspirin and put the dry mixture into the water bowl, and then stirred it up. Before long, the dog drank the water greedily, and within a half an hour the dog was out. John had some basic experience as a veterinarian from living on the farm all his life and had tended to a variety of animals.

John heated some water and cleaned the wound and afterward, he applied some anti-bacterial ointment to keep it from getting infected. He then sewed the wound up with a needle and some thread. "Well, it isn't a professional job, but it will do," he thought.

So, I got my newest and last name. And believe it or not; I liked it! I fell into a deep sleep and when I woke up, my back was stitched up and I felt much better, although I was still weak. I let John give me a bath and wash my face and head because I was unusually tired and groggy, and I didn't care. I even let him trim my hair.

After some weeks had passed, I was beginning to believe that John was the person that I was supposed to help. I began to get a little friendlier with him; just a little. As time went on, I began to like these two humans called John and Ed. I decided that I would hang around for a while, because I had nothing else to do and I was happy here. I figured I was never going to find my home and I had been gone so long now, that my memories of my beloved farm were beginning to fade; and it made me sad.

*Chapter Eighteen*

# Big John Goes To Heaven

inter turned into spring and the green leaves returned to the trees. The birds began to sing and each bird had its own song. The grass had turned green in the meadow and the multi-colored flowers began to pop out, stretching towards the life giving sun. The ice had melted off the pond, and the water began to ripple in the spring breeze and sparkle in the sunlight.

I had spent the winter with Big John and with the arrival of spring in the glen I was beginning to love it here with my new human. Big John and I would go walking everyday and in the evening we would drive the cows back home from the pasture. John would yell at them and they would start walking back towards the house, and I would help by barking at them. We made a great team and every once in a while I would let John pet my back; but that was it. John built a little trap door in the big door, so that I could come and go as I pleased.

When summer came and the days became hot, John and I would swim in the pond. The ducks would quack and fuss at us, splashing water everywhere and then make a bee line to the other side of the pond. But after awhile, they didn't mind us being in their bathtub.

In the evenings, John and I would set on the porch and watch the setting sun turn the sky red, pink, green, and gold, as the sun slowly disappeared behind the high dark mountains off to the west. Come nightfall, the stars would sneak out and sprinkle the vast night sky and the coolness of the night would set in. Sometimes Ed would sit with us on the porch. The frogs would begin their croaking down by the pond and the fireflies would come out at twilight and light up the entire valley, twinkling like hundreds of tiny stars. It was a peaceful time and we had fun; the three of us.

Sometimes, Ed would holler at the frogs to shut up and they would for about fifteen seconds, and then they would begin to croak again. Ed made us laugh and at those times, I would think to myself that the world was perfect and I was happy here with John and Ed. I was beginning to think that this was where I belonged.

Once in a while, I would ponder about my dream and I would think to myself that maybe John was the man I was supposed to help. I had no idea of what I was supposed to do, so I decided to hang out here and wait.

I spent all summer and into the late fall with John. Eventually, the green summer leaves began to change to gold, red, yellow, and brown. The air became cool and crisp and soon enough, winter had set in once again. I was glad to have a warm fire to lie beside. In the evenings, John would sit in his chair and watch TV and I would lie in my bed by the fire, full and content.

I was beginning to trust John and Ed and I felt more relaxed around them. I had decided to stay around here because I believed that John, or maybe Ed, was the one I was supposed to help. I could complete my special task and go back to Heaven. As the days went by, I had just about given up on ever finding my farm.

One late winter night, John and I were relaxing in the house as we usually did and the weather was extremely cold outside. The heat from the fire felt warm on my fur and as the fire crackled and hissed, I drifted off to sleep watching the orange, yellow, and blue flames dance around in the hearth.

When I woke up in the morning there was a bad smell in the house. I stood up and sniffed the air and what I smelled was one I faintly remembered on the farm when one of the animals had died. I looked around and sniffed again. I followed the smell and it led right to where Big John was sleeping in his chair. I barked at him and then sniffed him and I knew the smell was coming from him. I barked and pawed his chair but he didn't wake up and I noticed that he wasn't breathing. I went outside exiting through my little door and looked around for Ed, but he was nowhere in sight. I barked a couple of times and waited to see if Ed would show up; but he never came.

I went back inside after a few minutes and looked at John again, but he had not moved. I ate the little bit of food in the bowl and drank the rest of the water, until both bowls were empty. I went over to my bed by the fire and I lay down, staring at John.

I waited and watched all day to see if John would get up out of the chair, but he never moved and I knew that he was dead. I became overwhelmed with sadness because I knew that I would be leaving here soon and I wondered what awaited me, now that Big John was gone away. Maybe he went to Heaven, that place I had dreamed about with the strange human called Jesus.

When evening came, I looked out the bay window and I saw small white things floating from the sky. I wondered what they were and if they were dangerous because I had never seen these things before. I jumped up and placed my front paws on the window sill to get a better look in a standing position, with my face close to the window. I could feel the cold seeping through the window and the fire had gone out and it was getting cold in the house. I stared at the white things until darkness began to fall and I decided to go outside and investigate the strange white things.

I went to my little door and slowly pushed the swinging door open with my head, peering out cautiously until the door rose up enough for me to see past it. The white stuff was falling from the sky everywhere and it was on the ground too. The sky was an eerie white and it was extremely quiet outside. I looked around to make sure no one was outside and I slowly came out. I noticed that some of the white stuff had lain on the outside edge of the porch and on the steps. I walked over to the edge and sniffed the white stuff. It went up my nose and made me sneeze. It was very cold and I licked it, and it tasted just like water! I lapped up a good bit of it and then went back inside to find something to eat.

John had left the pantry door ajar and I opened it with my paw. I saw the bag of dog food and it made my mouth water. I swatted at the bag several times, but it didn't move. I got mad and jumped on the bag and started biting it with my teeth, tearing the bag. The bag fell out of the pantry and I managed to rip the bag open and food went everywhere. The little round balls of food were scattered all over the kitchen floor. I ate until I was full and then I went over and looked at John and he still hadn't moved. I was by myself and I was scared wondering what would become of me and I also wondered where the other human named Ed was.

I was there for three days, when a knock came on the door and I heard Ed's voice calling for John.

## Chapter Nineteen

# Leaving Big John

*E*d and Joanne had been at the hospital waiting on the delivery of their second grandchild. When they left the hospital they decided to go tell John the good news. When they arrived at John's house they got out of Ed's paint faded truck and walked up to the door. Ed rapped on the door. "John, you home?" There was no answer.

Ed called again loudly, "John! It's me, Ed."

I was sleeping on the couch buried in a blanket. The room was very cold and I had been trying to keep warm. I recognized Ed's voice and I heard another voice that sounded like a woman. I got off the couch and walked over to my little door and sniffed. Yes it was Ed, but I didn't recognize the other human's scent.

"Maybe he's out in the valley driving the cows back because of the snow," Joanne said.

"No, the cows are all here. I told him I wouldn't be around for a couple of days. He knew Dixie was due to deliver and that we'd be spending time with her at the hospital. Maybe he went into town for something," Ed surmised.

I stuck my head out and Joanne squealed. Ed laughed and said, "Easy honey! It's just BJ, John's little dog."

"He scared me. I wasn't expecting to see a head stick out of the bottom of the door. You guys have been busy. I didn't know John had a dog." she said laughing.

I jumped when the woman screamed, and I quickly ducked my head back inside. I turned and ran across the room as fast as I could, and hid underneath the couch.

"Hey BJ, come on out." Ed coaxed.

"Oh my God Ed, did you smell that odor when BJ stuck his head out the door? It smelled like something died in there. Pew!"

"Yeah, I smelled it," and it scared him. Ed began banging on the door and yelling, "John open up!"

"Don't you have a key?" Joanne asked worried.

"Yeah, but let's give John a couple of minutes to answer," he replied grimly.

"Ed, I got a bad feeling about this," she said.

Ed squatted down at the little door and called out for the dog. "BJ, come here boy. Is there something wrong BJ?" He could smell the odor and it was stronger down by the little trap door.

I came out from under the couch and barked a couple of times to tell them to come in, but they didn't. I heard Ed calling me, but I was scared they would think I made John dead and that they would want to hurt me, so I remained inside and I barked a couple more times. I was ready to go hide under the couch if they came in.

"Open the door Ed," Joanne commanded.

"Alright, we're coming in John!" Ed stated loudly to give John warning. Ed reached into his pocket and pulled out a set of keys, "Let's see... which one is it."

Joanne grabbed the keys out of Ed's hand and said, "For gosh sakes Ed, I've been telling you to get glasses for years now and you simply refuse to. You think you're still eighteen. When will you finally admit that you aren't young any longer?" she said disgustedly.

"I would have found it, I always do." Ed was stalling, because he knew in his heart that something was wrong.

"Ed, I don't think this is going to turn out good."

"Aw, John's probably in town." But Ed knew better and he was worried.

"Well, what's up with that horrible smell then?"

"Maybe BJ did his business in there while John was away."

"I never smelled dog poop that smelled that bad before," she said as she stuck the key in the lock. "Are you ready Ed?"

"I reckon so." Ed grimly answered. "Go ahead and open the door."

When they opened the door the stench hit them right in the face. They walked into the dark room and turned on the light and there sat John in his favorite chair dead as a doornail, and BJ was nowhere in sight.

I heard them coming in the door and I ran and hid under the couch, watching as they entered the room.

"Oh no," Joanne exclaimed as she saw John. "He's dead."

Ed felt a lump in his throat and he muttered, "Oh, John."

Joanne said, "We'll have to call the sheriff right away. Where's the dog at? We can take him to the shelter down the road. Doctor Vickie will know what to do with him."

Ed swallowed and said, "I suppose so. Couldn't we keep BJ? John really loved BJ and he's used to me."

"Ed, we've got more animals than we can take care of right now and we're not getting any younger," she replied with sympathy in her voice. She could tell that Ed loved the dog, but it was just too much for them. "We're getting too old for more animals Ed."

"BJ! BJ! Come here boy," Ed called.

I didn't hear anger in his voice so I decided to come out from under the couch. I stood in front of the couch in case I had to retreat back under it again. I stared at them and Ed squatted down and called me.

"Come on boy," Ed coaxed.

I walked over to him slowly and he petted me on the back. He knew not to get near my face, but I think at this point I would have let him pet my head because I was sad, and I knew they were too. I suddenly realized that I loved John and I was sure that they did too.

Joanne called the sheriff and in twenty minutes they arrived, along with an ambulance. The room began to fill with people and they were very busy. I watched them as Ed held me in his arms.

Ed said, "Come on BJ. Let's get outta here." He turned to Joanne and said firmly, "If nobody takes this dog and gives it a home, I'm taking him and I don't want to hear no fussing from you about it." Joanne knew better than to argue with him at this point.

"Ok Ed, but I'm sure Vickie will find him a good home. He's a cute little baby."

"Yeah, well don't nobody know him like I do. You gotta go easy with him, or he'll bite. He's been over the mountain and through the creek."

"What?" she asked.

"He's been badly abused," Ed said as if Joanne should have known what he meant.

"I've never heard it put that way Ed."

"Well by golly, you have now!" he said. He was upset. His best friend was dead and now he had to give little BJ away. What a rotten day this had turned out to be. The only bright spot was the arrival of his new grandchild.

## Chapter Twenty
# Among Old Friends

*E*d opened the front door to the shelter and walked in, followed by BJ on a leash. Heather was at the front desk and she greeted him saying, "What have we here." She recognized BJ right away and said, "Oh! It's the miracle dog!"

"You know this dog?"

"Yes, he's been in and out of here quite a few times. We call him the miracle dog."

"Why's that?"

"He was hit by a car and he died, but Doctor Vickie prayed over him and he came back to life."

"No kidding? He died and came back to life? Wow, I knew he was a tough one alright," Ed replied amazed. "You should have seen him when he was in that little cave, and me and Big John was trying to get him out. Boy that was a hoot!" Ed laughed and said, "I'm gonna miss this little fella. His name is BJ."

"Cave?" Heather asked confused.

"Never mind," Ed laughed and realized it was one of those things where "you had to be there". "He belonged to my friend Big John and he passed this morning. I don't have room for him, but if no one takes him call me, and I'll make room. "

"Ok," Heather said. "We'll take him from here. You said his name is BJ? We always called him Squirt."

"Yes, and remember if no one takes him, call me before you… you know. Just tell Doctor Vickie I'm Joanne's husband, Ed. She knows our number," he said.

Just then Doctor Vickie walked out to the front desk and saw the little dog and exclaimed, "I know this dog!"

"I hear he's known as the miracle dog." Ed said.

"Yes, he's been in and out of here quite a few times." Vickie said. She looked up at Ed and asked, "Aren't you Ed, Joanne's husband?"

"Why, yes I am. Are you Doctor Vickie?"

"Yes, I am. Pleased to meet you Ed." Vickie said.

She looked down at BJ puzzled, and asked, "Why did you bring the dog here and how did you come to acquire him?"

Ed related the story about finding BJ and about Big John's death. Then he told her that he had brought BJ here to the shelter, hoping they could find a good home for him. He then added that he would take BJ, if they couldn't find someone to adopt him.

"I'm so sorry to hear about your friend," she said sympathetically.

He nodded his head and said, "Now, don't forget to call me if nobody wants him."

Doctor Vickie said, "I definitely will Ed. Nice to meet you."

"Nice to meet you too," Ed responded.

"Good-bye BJ." Ed felt terrible letting BJ go.

"BJ? Is that his name?" Doctor Vickie asked.

"Yes." Ed explained that they had named the dog BJ, using Big John's initials.

"That's sweet. We always just called him Squirt," she said.

I was staring at Ed the whole time and I knew that he was about to leave me here, like everyone else had done. I didn't understand why Ed didn't want me anymore. I had been good and I only tried to bite him and John once or twice, when we first met. I thought we were getting along fine. Did he blame me for John's death?

Ed looked down at BJ and he felt sad for the dog. "Good-bye BJ," Ed said and he turned and went out the door feeling sad and depressed. He felt like a jerk leaving BJ there. He thought of how BJ had looked at him and he felt a lump in his throat.

I really didn't want to come back here, but here I was again. I guess Ed didn't want me. I thought that maybe he loved me, but I was mistaken. They put me in Old Blue's cell and that cheered me up somewhat, until I started missing him.

It wasn't long before most of the staff came to see BJ the miracle dog. BJ had no idea that he was famous and wondered why all these people were coming to stare at him. BJ spent the next three weeks in the shelter, until one day a man and his daughter came in looking for a small house dog.

Janet's father had two Great Danes, but they were much too big for her to play with. Janet was only eight years old and she wanted a small doggie. One that she could play with and that she could keep in her room.

Heather greeted them as they entered the door, "Hello, can I help you?"

Her father said, "Yes, we're looking for a small house dog for my daughter."

"Sure, we have several that you might like." She looked at Janet and asked, "What's your name sweetie?"

The little girl answered, "Janet."

"Well, let's go back to the kennel and you can look at all the doggies," Carmen said.

Carmen took them back to the kennel and they began to inspect each dog. Janet liked Sammy the little black and white Boston terrier, but when she saw BJ she fell in love. "Oh daddy he's soooo cute! Can I have this one?"

"I guess so," he sighed.

Janet's father's name was Jack and he didn't care much for small dogs. He looked at them as nothings. To him a big dog was more macho and you wouldn't dare catch him with a small dog, but for his daughter, he thought it was ok as long as it behaved.

He turned to Carmen and asked, "Can we get this one?"

"Sure, go back up to the front desk and we'll get the paper work completed and you can take him home," she said smiling at Janet.

"Does he have a name?" Janet asked.

"Yes his name is BJ and he's a special dog." Carmen replied.

Janet said, "Come on BJ I'm taking you home."

They bought a collar and leash at the shelter. Carmen put the collar on BJ, fastened the leash, and led him out to the front desk. Once the paper work was finished they left the shelter and Janet said, "Can I hold him in my lap daddy?"

"No, you need to be in your seat belt. We can put the dog in the back seat until we get home." They pulled out of the parking lot and drove home with BJ lying in the back seat. Janet was in the front seat anticipating the moment that she could play with her new dog.

I was somewhat nervous and scared because I didn't know what to expect. I wondered if this was the person I was supposed to help, like the man in the dream had said. And still, I wondered if the dream was real or not. Blue got a home, just like the man in the dream had promised and I thought that Big John was the one I was supposed to help, but I never helped John do anything. I was only beginning to trust him when he died. I was confused.

When they arrived at their house, Janet hopped out of the car. She opened the back door and put her arm around BJ's stomach, taking him out of the car, and placing him gently on the ground. "Come on BJ let's go for a walk in the yard."

Janet walked me around in the yard for a little bit and I noticed there were two big dogs on the deck. I wondered if I would have to stay with them outside on the deck. The dogs were staring at me and they wouldn't talk to me when we went up on the deck. I could tell they didn't like me.

"Come on BJ let's go to your new bedroom. It's really my bedroom, but now it's yours too."

I followed her into the house and we went down the hall to her bedroom. I was glad that I didn't have to be outside with those big dogs because they looked like a couple of sourpusses. I was there for only three weeks when Janet began to hurt me, twisting my ears and tail, and trying to tie bows in my fur and for some reason, little girls liked to put clothes on me, and I just hated that. I let her get away with it for a while, but it hurt and I had to do something to make her stop. My warning growls didn't seem to work, so I bit her finger. Not too bad; just a small bite. But that's all it took. I remembered then what Old Blue had said, "Humans can hurt us, but we aren't allowed to hurt them." It was good advise, but I wasn't about to let any human hurt me if I could help it.

Janet let out a loud scream and began crying.

Jack came in the room screaming at me and he began to beat me with his fists. He hit me five or six times and finally, he stopped, asking the little girl what had happened.

Janet said through her tears, "He...he...sob...b-b-bit m-me," and then she began to cry loudly again.

"Why you little mutt, that's it!" he threatened. "This dog stays outside from now on because he's too dangerous to be in here with Janet. Maybe I'll just shoot him and be done with it. I don't like the little whelp anyway. I'll get rid of him when I get the chance. I knew this was a bad idea."

Janet said, "I hate that dog! He' s mean to me."

Janet's mother consoled her saying, "We'll get you another dog sweetie. A good dog."

I looked around and there was no place to hide and the bed set too low to the ground, which left me at his mercy. He kicked me in the ribs several times and I felt intense pain and I yelped and whimpered. He took off his belt and began to whip me and all I could do was hope that he would stop, which he finally did. He took me outside onto the deck where the big dogs were and tied me to the deck railing on a short chain that was only about three feet long. My movement was restricted and I hated being tied up. I looked over across the yard and I saw a man standing on his porch looking at me. He probably wanted to hurt me too. I hated people. I was hurting from the pain and I had to lie down. I looked at the big dogs, but they just ignored me and I could tell that they thought they were better than me. I knew they didn't like me because of my small size.

Towards late evening, the man came out and unchained the bigger dogs and took them inside. Not long after that, the sun began to slip behind the far mountains and the sky had quickly turned to a dark purple. When the moon came up it was full and bright. The wind moved the dark clouds slowly across the winter sky, causing the moon to vanish, and then reappear. It was cold outside, and I was frightened and lonely.

I was on my own again.

## Chapter Twenty-One

# Bj Meets Dustin

*D*ustin was standing on his back porch enjoying his morning coffee. It was early March and winter was almost over, but it was still cold outside. His neighbor's back deck was fairly close to Dustin's porch and he had heard the neighbor's wife call him Jack, so Dustin assumed that was his name. He observed Jack bringing a little dog out of the back door and onto the deck. He watched as Jack chained the little dog up to the deck rail and Dustin noticed that it was a very short chain and he thought, "If that little dog slips or jumps off that deck, he'll hang himself. How stupid can you be, or is Jack doing it on purpose?"

Dustin could hear Jack yelling at the dog and it was apparent that his neighbor was angry about something; which seemed to be a regular habit for his neighbor. Dustin knew that Jack was a very unfriendly man and none of the other neighbors liked him because he had a violent way about him. He had cursed several of the people in the neighborhood for no good reason at all and had also cursed some children who had used his yard as a short cut.

Dustin watched as the man smacked the little dog once on the backside and he could hear the dog yelp. This made Dustin mad. He loved animals and he hated to see any animal being abused. To him, anyone that would abuse an animal, would abuse a child. He couldn't hear what Jack was saying to the dog and then Jack went inside, slamming the door. Dustin saw the dog look over at him and the dog stared at him defiantly and then the little dog lay down.

Dustin's wife Cassie came out on the porch and stood beside Dustin asking, "What are you looking at?"

Dustin said, "I saw our neighbor bring that little dog out," pointing at BJ. "He chained him to the deck railing and then he cussed the dog and hit him."

"I didn't think that guy liked little dogs. I thought he was more into the bigger dogs."

"I don't know he's a very strange man. I don't think that he cares much for animals. I think he only has those big dogs for protection, and I really believe that he could kill that little dog, and not think twice about it.

"His wife is strange too," Cassie added.

In the following weeks Dustin observed Jack beating the dog several times for no reason at all. He watched as the little dog fought for food and many times the bigger dogs kept him from eating at all. Any food that the little dog managed to get were the few morsels that had been accidentally spilled and rolled over his way, when the bigger dogs were eating. Dustin also noticed that the little dog was left tied up all day and night in any type of weather, while the big dogs were taken inside. Dustin grew madder by the day watching the little dog being treated in this manner. He heard Jack call the little dog "BJ" several times and Dustin assumed that was the dog's name. He thought, "That's a funny name."

One night he came home and it was raining hard. He decided to wait to see if the rain would let up, so he could run for the house. The night was pitch black and was momentarily lit up every few seconds by bright flashes of lightening, followed by loud booms of thunder. As the night lit up momentarily, Dustin looked over at Jack's deck and he saw the little dog jumping up at the door begging to be let in. He saw the porch light come on and Jack stepped out with a rolled up newspaper. He hit the dog several times in the face yelling for it to shut up, or he would shoot it. The little dog went over and huddled up against the wall of the house, shaking uncontrollably.

Dustin opened the car door and made a run for his house and went inside standing on the rug to drip off. He took off his coat and went to the kitchen window which faced Jack's back deck. He peered through the glass saying to Cassie, "Can you believe our neighbor has left that little dog out in this weather. I noticed the big dogs are inside where it's warm and dry."

"Are you serious?" Cassie said as she looked out the window. "Poor little thing."

"Does the dog do his business on the deck? Every time I see him he's on the deck."

"I see them take him out in the yard sometimes while you're at work. Other than that, he's always tied to the deck.

"And why in the world is he tied up on such a short chain. He could hang himself if he jumped off the deck. Did Jack do that on purpose? I don't care much for him hitting that poor little dog either. He's abusing that poor little animal. I heard him tell the dog that he was going shoot him."

The next night when Dustin came home from work he went into the kitchen and opened the refrigerator and took out a hamburger that was left over from the previous night's supper.

As he started out the door Cassie asked, "Where are you going with that hamburger?"

"I'm going to throw this meat to that little dog. If Jack won't feed him I will."

"Oh, no you're not," she said firmly.

"What?"

"That guy is crazy and he's liable to shoot you or something."

"It's midnight and the lights are off over there. I'll just toss it over on the deck and come back. I'll only be a second."

"Alright, but be careful because the moon is full and it's awful bright out there. He might see you. I'll go out on the porch and keep watch," Cassie said in a worried voice.

Dustin walked over to the deck and whispered, "Here boy," and gently tossed the meat onto the deck. The dog watched as the hamburger bounced and stopped near his paws. He then looked back at Dustin and stared at him without blinking. Dustin looked at the dog and saw that he was in horrible shape from being outside in the weather so long with no care, or companionship and it made him mad. His thoughts were interrupted when Cassie loudly whispered, "Dustin, get back here!"

Dustin turned and went back to his porch watching as the dog hungrily ate the meat. When the dog had finished eating he looked over at Dustin and stared. They looked at each other for a long time and finally Dustin went in and went to bed thinking of the little dog.

He felt sorry for the poor little thing. Why would someone treat an animal like that was beyond his comprehension. Should he call the police and report Jack?

Several days later it began to snow. It was a wet heavy snow, which was not unusual for early March. It began to stick to the ground and as the morning progressed the snow began to stick to everything. The snow had accumulated a little over an inch before stopping. It was Saturday and Dustin's brother Matthew had come over to visit, which he did quite frequently. The two brothers were close and they had grown up with a Boston terrier named Petie and they loved animals.

Dustin was looking out the kitchen window and he was getting madder by the second watching the little dog freezing in the snow. Matthew walked over to the window and peered out at the little dog asking, "Have they left that little dog out in the snow?"

"Yeah, look at him over there in the snow. The poor little thing is shaking from the cold. That man is an animal abuser. His name is Jack and I'd like to see him have to live outside on that deck day after day, and see how he likes it," Dustin said in disgust.

"It seems to me the whole family is heartless," Matt added.

"You're right. None of them cares about that poor little dog."

"Oh no!" Dustin hollered and he ran to the kitchen door, opened it and bolted out the door running towards Jack's deck.

Matthew was right behind him and Cassie asked, "What's wrong?" but when she looked out the window she could see that the little dog had slipped off the deck in the slippery snow and was hanging by his neck from the edge of the deck. The dog was too short for his legs to touch the ground and he was choking to death.

Dustin and Matthew ran as fast as they could in the snow. Dustin reached the dog first and grabbing it, he placed it back up on the deck. The little dog lay on the deck where Dustin had placed him and he was gasping for breath.

"We got here just in time," Dustin said out of breath.

"Is he alright?"

"I don't know. I think he's still alive."

"How stupid can you be?" Matthew said incredulously.

The dog gagged, coughed, and continued to breathe heavily.

I thought I was going to be dead, but that human helped me. He's the same one that gave me food one night. Maybe he is a good human.

Jack burst out of his back door and yelled, "What's going on out here! Why are you on my property?"

Dustin said, "Your dog slipped off the deck and was choking to death. We saved him."

"You should have let him hang. I'm calling the police." Jack replied.

"Go ahead buddy and we'll tell them how you've been treating this poor defenseless dog," Matthew replied staring at Jack with a serious look.

"What?" Jack said with a dumb look on his face.

Dustin chimed in and said, "I been watching you abuse this dog for quite a while, and I've seen enough. Call the police Matt."

Matt pulled out his phone as Jack's wife came out the door at that moment and she asked, "What's wrong Jack? What are they doing here?"

"These two idiots are trespassing, that's what's wrong," he said angrily. "Get off my land."

Matt said, "No, I think we'll just wait here for the police. We might get arrested for trespassing, but you'll go to jail for animal abuse."

Jack got mad and said, "I got a gun and I'll use it. Now get out of here!"

Dustin said, "Go ahead and get your gun and when the police get here they can arrest you for animal abuse *and* brandishing a loaded weapon."

Matt said menacingly, "Are you threatening us?"

Jack's wife looked at Matt and said, "Don't call the police." She turned to Jack and said, "If they are so concerned about that stupid dog, just give it to them. You were going to shoot him this weekend anyway. He's no use to us and it's costing us money to feed him."

"From what I've seen, you probably only spend ten cents a month feeding him," Dustin said sarcastically.

"Ain't nobody taking this dog. He's mine," Jack said stubbornly.

"Jack, just give them the dog and you can save a bullet and besides, if they take the dog it will be their problem. You can get payback when the dog rips their fingers off," she said looking at Dustin with a smile. Then she added, "He loves to bite."

"Say, I like that idea. If you want him you can have him, but I want the money it cost me to get him out of the shelter," Jack said. He thought he might as well make a little money on this deal. These two guys looked like a couple of bleeding hearts to him.

"How much do you want?" Matt asked.

Jack had only paid fifty dollars, but he figured he could make a profit and he answered, "Oh, let's see...how about seventy-five dollars."

Dustin looked at Matt without hesitating and said, "I only got fifty."

Jack said, "Well, I guess I'll have to shoot the mutt then. I can't take no less than seventy-five."

"I got the other twenty-five," Matt said giving Jack a dirty look.

They paid Jack his money and then Jack said, "You can come up here and get the mutt and I hope he bites the tar outta you." He laughed at the idea of the dog biting them and he stepped back to watch what would transpire.

Matthew asked, "What's the dog's name?"

"His name is BJ and he likes to bite," Jack said laughing.

BJ had recovered somewhat and had gotten to his feet. Dustin walked up on the porch and took the choker chain from BJ's neck. He petted the dog's back and then he put his arm under the dog's belly and picked him up carefully, not to let the dog's mouth get near his body. Dustin carried BJ back to his house with Matt following behind.

I only let this man pick me up because he gave me meat and he saved me from being dead; but mostly because he was taking me away from that crazy man named Jack. I didn't know where I was

going, but it had to be better than where I was. I thought maybe

this was the human I was going to help. I sure hoped so, because

I was getting awfully tired and I didn't know how much longer I

would last in this world of crazy humans.

Dustin and Matthew took BJ inside and got a blanket for him

to lie on by the electric heater and Cassie said, "I'll go out and buy

a bed, shampoo, dog food, and maybe a couple of toys for him this

afternoon."

I thought to myself that it felt so good to be inside a warm

house. I was so tired that I fell asleep immediately, not caring if

these humans planned to hurt me or not. I just didn't care anymore

and I no longer believed that my dream had any truth to it at all. It

was just a stupid dream.

Later that afternoon BJ had a nice soft comfortable bed to lie in.

Dustin put the new bed by the electric heater and then they filled

up the plastic dog bowls with food and water. They sat in the living

room and watched the dog sleep while they discussed how to clean

him up without getting bit.

When I woke up, the humans were outside and I went to the

window and watched them. They were in the white cold stuff with

brooms cleaning off their cars. I wondered if they were going to take me back to jail and I really didn't want to go. It was lonely there without Blue and I didn't have any friends there anymore. I wanted to stay here. I don't know why, but I just did. I went back and lay in the bed by the heater, wondering what they were going to do with me.

I sat and watched as the humans came back in and took their coats off. They sat down on the couch and began talking to each other. I just lay there and stared at them. I learned that the one who had saved me was called Dustin, and the other two were called Matt and Cassie.

Later that afternoon, they decided to take a chance at cutting BJ's hair. They managed to cut some of the long hair around his paws, his body, and even a little around his face. BJ only snapped at them a couple of times. He missed several times, but he connected with Dustin once.

It wasn't a bad bite, and Dustin told Matt and Cassie that it did hurt a little, but he was alright. When they finished, BJ looked somewhat better and then they decided to give him a bath. They filled the tub with warm water and placed him in the tub. Cassie took a plastic drinking cup out of the cabinet and they used it to pour water on BJ. They squirted shampoo on him and washed everything behind his head. Cassie squirted some shampoo in the cup and mixed it with water and poured the mixture over BJ's head. After that, she rinsed his head. Cassie said, "There, now you're all clean." They dried him with a towel, but left his head and face area alone.

Dustin and Cassie had BJ for almost a month when a phone call changed everything.

## Chapter Twenty-Two

# Bj Moves One More Time

*D*ustin and Matthew's father Patrick was sixty years old. He had no grey in his hair, and he looked much younger than his age. He was short and stocky and had more energy than a teenager. He loved animals with a passion and he believed that they had souls, and were just as loved by God as any human being. As a matter of fact; he trusted animals more than he did humans. When Patrick was forty-one he had been in a bad motorcycle accident and his back had been broken in two places. All the doctors were amazed that he could still walk. Five doctors told him that according to the X-rays, he should be at the very least, paralyzed and in a wheel chair. Patrick was a tough man, but he had a big heart. He had been badly abused both physically and mentally by his alcoholic father. His mother had stood by and watched him being abused, which only enabled his father to continue the abuse.

The verbal abuse had continued long after Patrick had grown into a man and he had finally cut off all ties with his parents.

Patrick had one problem; he had a hard time forgiving people who had done him wrong. Sometimes he thought of his father and wished that things could have been different, but Patrick had grown up hard and he was well aware that wishes were a waste of breath. He had cut off all relations with his father and mother for almost ten years. His only family was his wife Marie and his two sons, Matthew and Dustin.

At the age of fifty-three Patrick had a major heart attack that required five stents and he spent a week in the hospital. The doctor told him he couldn't understand how Patrick had made it to the hospital, because most people in his condition would never have made it to the hospital in the shape that he was in. Patrick confided in his wife and sons that he had had a spiritual experience while in the hospital. After that, he had become a Christian and devoted his life to God. He gave God all the credit for surviving his near death events whereas before, he thought it was his toughness that had gotten him through.

Dustin and Cassie had applied to rent an apartment and the renters had called and told them they could move in the following week, but pets weren't allowed in the building. That left Dustin with no choice but to take BJ over to Patrick's house to see if his father would take BJ in. He knew that it was probably BJ's last chance, because nobody wanted a dog that bites; except Patrick. Dustin knew his father would not refuse to take BJ in no matter what. He felt bad imposing on him, but it was either that, or BJ would probably be killed.

Dustin picked me up and I knew he was taking me away. I knew it wouldn't last. They were finally getting rid of me. They put me in the car and we went off down the road. At first I thought we were going back to jail, but we didn't go in that direction. By now, I knew the way to the jail and I was perplexed and a bit worried. I thought that maybe they were taking me back to the woods and drop me off, but then we pulled up to a strange house and Dustin took me out of the back seat of the car and carried me in the door.

When we entered the house, he set me down on the floor and for some odd reason I had a strong urge to go straight into the other room. When I entered the big room I saw a man sitting in a chair and I stopped and stared at him. There was something completely different about him. What was it? I was very curious as to why I was drawn to this human. I'm sure he was just like the rest and I noticed that he looked a lot like the one called Dustin. I stood there and stared at this man and wondered what it was about him that drew me to him. For some reason I felt no fear with this man and somehow, I knew that this was the person I was supposed to help. I didn't know how I knew; I just knew.

Patrick was sitting in the living room watching television when he heard Dustin and Cassie come in the house. He could hear Marie talking to them in the kitchen when he noticed something to his right, and when he turned and looked down, there was a little dog standing there staring at him.

"Well hello there. Where did you come from?" Patrick asked smiling.

BJ just stared at Patrick.

Dustin walked in and said, "Oh, you two have already met."

"Yes we have, where did he come from? You never told me you had a dog."

"We only had him for about a month or so, but we got a small problem."

"What's your problem?"

"Well...I need a favor from you," Dustin said.

"What is it? We'll see if we can fix your problem."

Dustin pointed at BJ and replied, "That's the problem."

"What do you mean?"

"The rental agency called and said we could have the apartment we applied for, but they don't allow pets. If we take him to the shelter they will probably kill him. I don't think anyone will take him and if they do, they'll bring him back after he bites them. They will more than likely kill him."

"He bites does he?" Patrick asked smiling.

"He's been abused a lot and he likes to bite."

"He's a cute little thing," Patrick said, feeling a kinship with the little dog already.

"I was hoping you could take him in Dad," Dustin pleaded. "He was being abused by my neighbor and we rescued him, and now we can't keep him because they don't allow pets where we're moving to."

"What? You know who was abusing him? What's his name? I'll have him arrested." Patrick said angrily sitting up in the chair.

"No Dad calm down, it's alright. We saved the dog and that's the important thing." Dustin knew that his father used to have a temper and was aware that he had changed, but he knew that his dad still got mad about certain things; and animal and child abuse was one of them. His Dad had suffered a heart attack not long ago and he didn't want him getting upset.

"Well, you should have had him arrested," Patrick said. He looked down at the little dog and said, "You need a home little one? We'll get along just fine because I know all about abuse, and I know how it feels. I don't blame you for biting humans; they probably deserved it."

BJ just stared at him and Patrick asked, "Is he ok?"

"Yeah Dad, he's just been badly abused and he probably thinks that I'm abandoning him. We've made some headway with him and I think he's starting to trust us."

"Sure, we'll take him in and he can still see you when you come over. Maybe that will help with the trust issues if he can see you here sometimes."

"Great! Thanks Dad," Dustin said with relief. "I'm sorry I had to spring this on you."

"Does your mother know?"

"Yeah, she said she's its ok with her, but to ask you too."

"So...I guess I got a new dog named BJ. It has been lonely since Petie passed."

"Where did he get the name BJ?"

"I don't know. That's what the owners said his name was."

He looked at BJ and said, "You want to stay with me BJ?"

I just stared at him, wondering what was different about him. I had the same feeling with Dustin, but this feeling was much stronger and I remembered my dream. Maybe…just maybe, this man was the one. Yes! I felt it in my spirit, just like the man called Jesus told me I would. This man had to be the one!

After Dustin and Cassie left, Patrick stared at the little dog and a strange feeling came over him. He didn't understand, or know what the feeling was, but he felt a strange kinship to this particular animal. He shook it off and chalked it up to losing their last dog Petie, who had passed a year prior to BJ's arrival. They had Petie for fifteen years and his death had crushed Patrick and his wife.

Patrick looked down at the little dog, and BJ continued staring at him. Patrick chuckled and asked, "You hungry?"

Patrick had no idea of the extraordinary events that were about to unfold.

## Chapter Twenty-Three
# God Takes Bj Home

O ver the next few months BJ had bitten Patrick on a few occasions. They weren't bad bites, but the last one was worst of all. It was a bad bite and it required stitches, but Patrick put off going to the hospital because he was afraid that they might try to take BJ from him; or, they would more than likely be required by law to put him down. The laws had changed and the state required that all dog bites had to be reported to the authorities. Finally, Patrick had to go to the hospital because the bite had become infected and his hand had swollen up. The doctor knew that it was a dog bite and Patrick could not hide this fact.

Just as he feared, they called the Animal Control Office and sure enough, a control officer showed up at the hospital. Patrick begged and pleaded with the officer and related the history of abuse the dog had suffered. The officer finally consented to let Patrick keep the animal, but put him and BJ on parole. BJ was not allowed to go off Patrick's property and he had to be on a leash when outside. Patrick had to call in every day for a week and report to the officer, as to the dog's behavior. The last stipulation was that if the dog bit anyone else, it would have to be disposed of. Patrick jokingly asked the officer, "Do you need to take a mug shot of me and BJ?"

When Patrick came home, he ignored BJ and only spoke to him in order to scold him. Patrick did this for three days and he could see that BJ was sorry. After that, he just knew in his heart that BJ would never bite him again.

I wish I hadn't of bit Patrick. It was just an old habit I guess. I figured he would take me to jail or hit me; but he didn't and I was surprised. Patrick just pointed to the place where I bit him, telling me that I was "bad" in a loud voice. But he didn't take me away and he never hit me. This was not normal human behavior and I realized that I really liked Patrick; no, I realized that I loved him and I loved it here in this house. I had been here so long now that I was used to it and Dustin would come and visit me sometimes too. I wanted to stay here more than I wanted to be on my beloved farm. I realized that I wanted to be with Patrick.

In the short following months after the hospital trip, Patrick and BJ became the best of friends and Patrick knew in his heart that BJ would never bite him again. God had told him this in his spirit. He knew that God wanted to test his forgiveness and to see how much Patrick really loved animals. Unbeknownst to Patrick, God had a job for him.

Eventually, BJ and Patrick were stuck together like glue and everyone in the family was surprised at the turn in BJ's behavior. Patrick could pick BJ up and hold him like a baby and kiss his cheek; and BJ would let him, but only Patrick was allowed this privilege and no one else. At night when they went to bed, BJ would lick Patrick's ear and then snuggle down beside him in the bed. The two went everywhere together and spent many nights out back enjoying a campfire, which BJ loved. Patrick would pull the swing up close to the fire and put a blanket around BJ and they would spend hours together in warm or cold weather. They played fetch and tug of war with BJ's toys and sometimes they would go for a ride in the car. BJ loved going for a ride in the car and he would stick his little head out of the window, watching all the cars and people as they went by, breathing the fresh air.

BJ and his new family went camping and they swam and played in the lake. On occasion, Patrick would take his canoe to the creek and he and BJ would float down the creek just relaxing, as the current took them downstream, slowly meandering in the warm sun and slipping through the shade of the overhanging trees. BJ had finally found love and a good home and he and Patrick had become inseparable. They were best friends and wherever Patrick was; so was BJ.

One morning BJ fell on the floor and had a spasm, which lasted only thirty seconds or so. Over the following weeks, it got to the point where sometimes BJ wasn't able to walk, or stand on his own. One Saturday morning, Patrick woke up and noticed that there was a small amount of blood in BJ's right eye. Patrick helped BJ out of the bed, setting him on the floor when suddenly, BJ fell over on his side onto the floor and began thrashing around for several seconds. It scared Patrick to death and he rushed BJ to the hospital. When he and BJ arrived at the hospital Doctor Toby took BJ back into the clinic for an examination. Patrick was beside himself because he knew it was serious. Patrick sat there alone waiting for the Doctor to return, thinking the worse. Tears began to form in his eyes.

He had been waiting for half an hour wondering what was going on, when Doctor Vickie finally came out. Patrick stood up and Dr. Vickie told him to sit down because she wanted to talk to him.

"Doctor you got to help BJ he's a special dog. My son rescued him from his neighbor and I know he suffered some abuse, but there was something about him that I just can't put my finger on.

I've owned dogs and other animals before, but there is just something unique about BJ. I don't expect you to understand, but please do whatever it takes to help him," Patrick pleaded with wet eyes.

"I wasn't going to tell you this, but since you've told me that, I feel that you should know something about BJ,"

"What is it?"

"Did you know he was in and out of this shelter quite a few times before you gave him a home?"

Patrick shook his head. "No, I didn't."

"He's been through a lot more abuse than you and your son are aware of. Almost all the people who took him out of here abused him and threw him out of their house. Most of them were too cowardly to bring him back for adoption. They just dumped him somewhere to die, but the poor thing kept showing up here. Do you know how he got his name?" she asked.

"No."

"A man named Big John found him near the mountains in a little cave that BJ had managed to crawl into after he had been left in the freezing cold, shot, and half starved. A mountain lion was trying to claw his way into the hole to get at him when luckily, Big John found him. John rescued him and took him in and he had BJ for almost two years. John gave him his initials as a name and that's how he got the name BJ. However, something extraordinary happened here at the clinic involving BJ." She hesitated to let this all sink in.

"What happened?" Patrick was dumbfounded at hearing all this.

"Sometime before John found him he was hit by a car. A young couple found him and brought him here and he actually died right here in this clinic."

"He died?" Patrick said amazed.

"…And he came back to life. He is more than a special dog and I just wanted to let you know that," she said.

"Wow. That's amazing. Thanks for telling me that Doctor. You're right, I needed to know that. I knew there was something about him that was strangely unique. I could sense that the first time I met him. So, BJ died and came back to life. Praise God. Thank you for telling me this Doctor."

Doctor Vickie then sighed a deep breath and said, "I'm just going to tell you straight out. This time, his luck has run out."

Patrick felt as though someone had punched him in the stomach. He couldn't hold the tears back any longer and long wet tears streaked down his cheeks. "There's nothing you can do?"

"I'm afraid not, he has a brain tumor." She then said sympathetically, "His head was damaged in the car accident and I'm sure that was when the tumor began. I'll give you some medicine to take home to ease his pain until he passes."

Patrick covered his face with his hands and shaking his head, as the tears started falling faster. Then he said in a whisper, "How long has he got? He's not that old."

"I don't know. Not long, it's pretty advanced," she said softly. "I'm sorry. He was a very special little dog." Then she said hesitantly, "If you want we can…"

"No! I'm taking BJ home with me Doctor. I'll not leave him by himself. BJ will die with me by his side." Patrick firmly stated.

Vickie nodded and went to get the medications leaving Patrick alone. A few minutes later, Doctor Toby brought BJ out to where Patrick was sitting. Doctor Toby handed BJ to Patrick and he took him in his arms.

Doctor Toby said, "You know, we called this little dog the miracle dog. He died once and God gave him a second chance. You were lucky to know him. He is God's special dog." and he turned and left.

Patrick watched Doctor Toby walk away.

Doctor Vickie came back with three medications and explained how to administer each one. Patrick left the hospital and took BJ home and laid him in his little bed by the heater and then he told

Marie the bad news. He related to Marie the story about how BJ had died at the shelter and had come back to life.

I wasn't feeling well and Patrick took me to see Doctor Vickie. I think I heard them say I was going to die, and I knew by now what that meant. I had forgiven humans and realized that there were a few good ones. I was going to miss Patrick, Marie, Dustin, Cassie, and Matt. This made me very sad to know that I had to leave my human family. I really wanted to stay here for a while longer because I finally found love and a good home, and now I had to leave. But I knew I was going to Heaven and I knew it was time to go, because I could feel it in my spirit. My task was finished and I had helped the person that Jesus had sent me to help, and I felt that my time was up here on earth. But I also knew that Patrick and my human family would join me in Heaven someday soon, and that we would all be together forever.

Patrick was not about to leave BJ by himself. That night as always, he placed BJ in the bed with him and Marie and he lay down beside him, with BJ curling up beside Patrick.

"We've had a great time old friend." Patrick told BJ. He talked to BJ for a long time, reminiscing about all the good times that they had shared together, and BJ quietly listened.

I felt bad and I was weak. I could hear Patrick talking to me and I knew much of what he said. I remembered many of the times that he was talking about and it made me happy remembering those good times. I loved Patrick and my new family, but I knew I was leaving. Eventually I began to fade and I began to see a bright light. I could see the bridge now. Rainbow Bridge.

Sometime during the night they both fell asleep. BJ passed during the night and when Patrick woke up and discovered that BJ had passed, he broke down and cried uncontrollably. Marie tried to console him, but it was no use. For days Patrick cried and he tried everything he could to get BJ's death off of his mind, but he couldn't stop thinking of his little buddy.

One day Marie said, "What is wrong with you Patrick? BJ had a great life here with us and he was loved as much as anyone could be loved. He spent his last years living like a king. He's in Heaven now and you have to accept it."

"But I can't, it's killing me, because I have to know if he's really in Heaven, or not. I feel like part of me is gone. I'm empty inside and nothing I do helps. I have to know if he's in Heaven, or just a pile of dust."

"Then pray about it."

"I have been for almost three weeks. I've been praying, begging, and even demanding to know where my little buddy is; but the Lord won't tell me."

Marie folded her arms and looked Patrick right in the eyes. "Then pray for three more weeks," she said with finality.

Patrick went into the living room and started praying as hard as he could for a solid hour and he heard nothing. He lay back in his chair wondering what was wrong with him, because he had never been so broke up about the death of a dog before. Sure, he was really hurt when Petie passed, but there was something different about BJ. There was something special about BJ that he did not understand.

Suddenly, the room fell away and Patrick found himself in a beautiful field full of flowers and lush green grass. The flowers were colors that he had never seen before and when he looked up, there was BJ and he was young and vibrant looking. When BJ saw Patrick he ran to him and leapt into his arms licking his face. Patrick hugged him and told him that he missed him and loved him and BJ answered him back telling him that he loved, and missed him too.

Patrick saw Jesus standing a few feet away smiling. Jesus allowed them some time together and then Jesus took BJ in his arms and told Patrick. *"I love my animals and I know you do too.*

*I know you're wondering why you have grieved over BJ so much. It is because I intensified your love in order to make you pray and ask me to bring you here to see him. I used your love of BJ to bring you here to tell you that forgiveness is the most important thing you can do. You must have unconditional forgiveness and uncondi- tional love, like a dog. Like me. You have a black spot in your heart Patrick that needs to be removed. It is the black spot of unforgive- ness of your father. You must release it and cleanse your heart. I know that sometimes it is hard for you to forgive and I wanted to stress to you how important forgiveness is. I also wanted you to know that I love my animals and that they do go to Heaven. I have chosen you to let the world know how much I love my animals. You will tell the world that they have spirits and that they go to Heaven to be with me when they pass."*

Patrick asked, "How Lord?"

And the Lord said, *"You will write a book telling the world about my great love for my animals."*

"Me? Write a book? I don't know anything about writing a book Lord."

*"I will direct you how to go about it and I will give you all the scriptures to prove that I love my animals. There has been a rise in the abuse of my animals on the earth and I am very angry about it.*

189

*I want you to let people know that it is a sin to mistreat my animals and now, I will give you a little more time with BJ, and then you must go back. I wanted you to know that BJ is with me and that you do not have to grieve any longer. When you die you will be reunited with BJ here forever. BJ is with me in Heaven. Grieve no more."*

Then Jesus disappeared. Patrick and BJ talked for several minutes and then BJ told Patrick that he loved him, and would see him soon in this very field; in Heaven. Then BJ said good-bye and he disappeared into a strange golden mist.

In the blink of an eye, Patrick found himself back in his chair. He wished he would have had more time with BJ, but his grief had been replaced with joy. He told his wife and sons what had happened and they were happy to know that BJ was truly in Heaven. They believed Patrick because they knew that their father would never joke about something like that. Marie told him that she knew God would not let him, or BJ down.

Patrick stayed true to the task that Jesus had given him. He told everyone he knew that God had showed him that animals went to Heaven and he didn't care if anyone believed him or not. Patrick forgave his father and God then directed him to write a book about all that had happened, telling the whole world that God loves His animals, and that they do go to Heaven.

## Chapter Twenty-Four
# Back To The Begining

*S*o that's my story. I died young, but I don't mind because now I'm in Heaven with all family and I'm just waiting for Patrick to join me. He was here once to visit me, but Jesus made him go back again just like I had to. But I know that he's coming back soon and Jesus said that he will get to stay here with me forever. Patrick and I only had a short time on earth, but when he comes back this time, it will be for good and we will be together forever and ever. That was my task. I had to die in order to bring Patrick here, so Jesus could tell him about forgiveness. That was my special job.

I completed my destiny and I helped the person I was supposed to help. Jesus said I had to go through all the abuse I went through, because Patrick had been abused too. The abuse made us compatible for each other, so that Jesus could teach me and Patrick about forgiveness. Jesus kept His promise and I get to live here forever and I get to keep my name BJ too. Everybody here calls me BJ; even Jesus.

Oh I forgot to tell you! Please don't tell the other animals, but I got more rewards and gifts for completing my mission than they did.

Heaven is great because there's no pain, no sadness, no hunger, and no death. My Mom, Dad, Charlie, and Co-Co are here and Jesus said that all my brothers and sisters would be along soon. There are all kinds of animals here too and we all get along just fine. Even those crazy pigs are here.

I come down to Rainbow Bridge often looking to see if Patrick has arrived yet. I know Marie, Matt, Dustin, and Cassie will be along eventually too. I can't wait!

And I get to see Big John whenever I want because he's here too. Oh, and look who else is here!

"How ya doin' kid?"

# A Note From The Author

Animals have feeling just like we do. They get cold, hungry, thirsty, and they also need companionship and love.

All dogs come from wolves which are their ancestors. Most dogs have been cross-bred by man and are not made for extreme weather conditions. Small dogs especially are not made to stay out in the cold.

People think of the Alaskan Husky and believe that all dogs can stay out in the cold. First of all Husky's huddle together under the snow which gives them insulation, and secondly there are four or more that huddle together to stay warm. A domesticated dog or cat cannot take the winter cold or the summer heat. Basically, they are the same as we are. If you can't take being out in a dog house in the cold, or in a hot car; neither can an animal.

Wild animals have their own ways to protect themselves from the elements which are God given; and their environment allows them to find or build a proper shelter. Domesticated animals don't have that luxury.

Please take your pets inside during cold and hot weather temperatures, because they are just like us. Anything else is abuse.

# About The Author

Steven Woodward was born in Houston, Texas and has lived in several states in the south but now resides in West Virginia with his wife of 35 years. He enjoys hobbies such as playing guitar and banjo. Steven spent four years in the United States Navy as a Communications Technician and graduated from Shepherd University in 2001 with a Psychology degree; graduating with full honors at the age of 40 and was inducted into two Honor Societies. Steven has published two pieces of literature in the Sans Merci at Shepherd University. He is the father of two wonderful sons and has four precious grandchildren. Steven has a Cairn terrier named Jasper and he is spoiled rotten.

# Other books by Steven Woodward:

"*Biblical Proof Animals Do Go To Heaven*" By Steven H. Woodward, 2012

"*God's Revelations Of Animals And People*" By Steven H. Woodward, 2017

Visit Steven Woodward's Facebook Page at: Steven Woodward or visit the link below:

https://www.facebook.com/profile.php?id=100010267894532

Steven Woodward's books can be purchased at: amazon.com/ barnesandnoble.com/audible.com

CPSIA information can be obtained
at www.ICGtesting.com
Printed in the USA
LVOW10s0141250518
578413LV00016B/189/P